04534

CU00904409

RHS

Night Train to Utah

Night Train to Utah

JACK REASON

A Black Horse Western

ROBERT HALE · LONDON

ISBN 0 7090 6629 5

Robert Hale Limited
Clerkenwell House
Clerkenwell Green
London EC1R 0HT

This for J and S

Typeset by
Derek Doyle & Associates, Liverpool.
Printed and bound in Great Britain by
WBC Book Manufacturers Limited, Bridgend.

ONE

They punched and kicked him from the smoke-hazed depths of Mahooney's bar to the street, dragged him more dead than alive to Jessom's corner store, and were a whole three minutes getting him to his feet for the short stumble to the lantern glow at the last building far end of town.

Not a deal of his once sharp broadcloth coat and fancy-fronted shirt, lean, tanned features and ice-blue eyes were still recognizable beneath the blood and dirt when Sheriff Hendy finally opened the door to his office and stepped to the pool of yellow light to stare like a bored, sulking dog at an offering of bad meat.

'Well,' he drawled, rolling a twist of chewing baccy round his mouth, 'what yuh got?'

'Heap of dung here, Mr Hendy,' spat one of the dozen men surrounding the mound of rags. 'Dealin' a marked deck back there at Mahooney's. Billy Soon caught him red-handed. Plain as day.'

'And he ain't laid one bit to Lacy Alice in payment for the pleasure of her favours neither,' snapped another, twisting the man's arm into his shoulder blades. 'That so, fella?'

The man groaned and vomited a clot of blood.

'Tell yuh somethin' else,' clipped a bony-faced fellow with a flickering squint in one eye, 'he's got a horse hitched at Mac's livery which he ain't no right to. Nossir. Clancy Springs says as how he slipped it from his corral out there at Nape Sands two days back. Scumbag reckons he won it fair in a five-stud game. T'ain't so. No way.'

'That's horse-stealin', Mr Hendy,' croaked a man, scratching his exposed belly. 'Fella could hang for that.'

Hendy widened his glare but said nothing.

'Gotta lip on him like a snivellin' whore along of it,' sneered a bowler-hatted streak of a fellow with loose braces and a ginger stubble. 'Been insultin' the town. Said as how Peaceway brought to mind some two-bit left-over sloshin' in a hog's pen. Said that he did, sonofabitch!'

The men grunted, cursed and closed menacingly on the mound.

'Ain't for havin' the likes of him about, Mr Hendy,' said bony face. 'Peaceway ain't no place for him. Reckon yuh should jail him and git to settlin' with him come sun-up.'

'String him up now, damnit!' snapped the scratcher. 'Get it done with. Don't hold to horse-thieves, not here, not no place.'

'Done it before, ain't we?' murmured a dapper little man screwing his eyes behind ill-fitting spectacles. 'Did it for Frank Neers, and that rat-faced vermin name of Grimms. Sure we did. And Pete Gregory when he rode along of the Packer mob. Gotta keep the town clean, ain't we, Mr Hendy? Ain't that what yuh've always said?'

'This fella got a name?' asked the sheriff through an oozing chew on the wad of baccy.

'Brown,' said the man twisting on the fellow's arm. 'Just that. Just Brown.'

'From?' frowned Hendy, aiming a line of spittle to the mound's blood-smeared boots.

'Ain't said, not yet. Just rode in outa the Sands. Yuh want my opinion—'

'I don't. I ain't askin',' said Hendy, shifting his weight and levelling his gaze.

' 'Course yuh ain't,' grinned ginger-stubble, stretching his braces. 'T'ain't opinions Mr Hendy wants; it's facts. Can't bring down the law without facts, can yuh? But we got plenty of them, no mistake.'

'I know the law,' grunted Hendy. 'I *am* the law.' His gaze moved over the faces. 'Don't ever get to thinkin' other. T'ain't healthy.'

'Sure, sure,' murmured the men, dragging the mound upright, pulling on his hair to lift his bruised, battered face to the high night sky.

'Yuh got a space for this scum back there, Mr Hendy?' mumbled the dapper man, adjusting his spectacles. 'Mebbe along of that Jameson fella yuh holdin'? Two rats in the same pen. Hell, this rate we're goin' to need a bigger jail!'

Hendy stared the man into silence, rolled the chewing baccy and shifted his weight again. 'I got the space. I always got the space. Whole point of my job here, ain't it? But there ain't goin' to be no hangin', not t'night.'

The men groaned their disappointment.

'Yuh goin' to have to wait on that. Yuh hear me?' snapped Hendy.

'We hear yuh, Mr Hendy,' said ginger stubble. 'Hear yuh good, but how come?'

'Well, seein' as how yuh all bein' so public spirited here and lookin' like yuh always are to keepin' Peaceway decent as it is, I'll tell yuh.' The men fell silent under Hendy's gaze. 'We gotta certain Marshal Quaid visitin' us. Big time lawman from Utah way; real important, so I hear, and tough as they come on the detail of law-makin' and upholdin' it. Know what I mean? Yuh got me?'

Hendy's stare narrowed. The baccy rolled noisily. 'I *mean*, case it's escapin' yuh, the marshal ain't for messin' with – so, when he rides in here noon t'morrow he's goin' to see and hear a town as tidy and law-abidin' by the book as he's witnessed this side of the Colorado. Ain't goin' to be so much as a boot or a word outa place. Yuh don't look at the fella, none of yuh, save to bid him time of the day, and yuh don't speak to him neither. I make m'self clear? He just rides in, takes himself a while to eat and freshen up, then leaves on the night train to Utah, Jameson shackled to him tighter than a tick.'

'That why he's comin', to collect Jameson?' asked the squinting man.

'That's precisely why,' said Hendy, aiming another line of spittle to the dirt. 'Jameson leaves here as the marshal's prisoner, shippin' out to stand his trial at Morriston, and I personally don't give a damn to the outcome, save that the murderin' sonofabitch hangs high as we planned for him here and that Peaceway under *my* law-keepin' goes into the record as havin' brought the rat to book clean, lawful and in style.' The sheriff's glare flashed. 'First man who scuffs the boardwalk, so to speak, gets to answerin' to me

minute that train pulls out. Law-keepin' here stands
to me, my way, my say-so, my doin'. Let's hold to that,
eh?'

'Oh, we ain't for arguin', Mr Hendy,' smiled loose
braces. 'Nossir, that we ain't. Wouldn't have it no
other way. Your town, your style. Fella sleeps easy in
his bed in Peaceway.' The men murmured their
agreement. 'So what we do about this scum?'

'Well, now,' grinned Hendy, 'seein' as how yuh
all buzzin' for puttin' that hangin' tree to use, and
seein' as how I ain't for lettin' yuh down, we'll
clean up Mr Brown here – make him look like
somethin' livin' and bein' dealt with proper for the
benefit of our visitin' Marshal – then, soon as we
seen the last of that night train, we'll have ourselves
a party, eh? We'll hang the sonofabitch Peaceway
style!'

'That's more like it, Mr Hendy!' yelled the
scratcher.

'Yuh got it, Mr Hendy!' sniggered loose braces.

'Good,' smiled Hendy, rolling the baccy fast and
easy. 'So yuh get to it, will yuh? Clean the fella up real
fresh. And when yuh done that, have Mahooney send
me a bottle and that pretty-lookin' half-breed gal he's
got tucked away.'

'Yuh got that too, Mr Hendy. You bet!'

It was only then, when the pool of yellow light had
faded, the door to Hendy's office thudded shut, the
street emptied of the men and the mound of blood-
soaked rags, and a moonlit silence settled over
Peaceway, that the figure in the shadows drew on the
cheroot and slid a thin wisp of smoke to the sultry
night air.

He had seen and heard all he needed. Now he knew exactly what to do.

TWO

Dubs Mahooney was having a fit of the snake eyes. He was being watched; something, or somebody, was out there, or maybe right here in the backroom to the bar, but somewhere close, in any one of a dozen dark corners where the shadows waited.

Been there some time too, he reckoned, since the last of the drinkers had staggered through the batwings, the poker players slouched away to their empty beds, the girls dragged their bodies to cold, lifeless rooms and Beanstalk finally got to his odd jobs around the place and mopped the smeared bloodstains from the bar and boardwalk.

Not done much of a job neither, he thought, steadying his grip to pour himself another measure from his private bottle, marks were still there, black as the shadows. You looked real close you could make out the prints of the man's hands.

He shuddered, downed the drink in one gurgling gulp and blinked on the sweat at his eyebrows. Boys had sure as hell gone to town on that fellow Brown. Beaten him to within a splinter of a pine box and a sun-up ride to Boot Hill – which is where he was destined, anyhow, come another few hours, minute

11

that visiting marshal had loaded his prisoner aboard the night train and waved his farewell.

He shuddered again and reached for the empty glass. Hendy was pushing it tight, he thought, running his luck and his hold on the town to the limit. Damn it, there would be another hanging almost before folk had blinked on the last one.

Another liquor-fazed march to the hanging tree, the shouting, jeering, yelling, women and young ones going along of it, most too gut-wrenched with fear to back off. Hendy would stand there, judge and jury; somebody would begin a hymn, somebody belch and the frenzy gather like a swarm till the body dangled limp as sodden baggage and the mob stood silent and Peaceway, as Hendy would pronounce in his best preacher-black tones, could sleep easy.

Once again. Till the next stranger rode into town and stepped easy to the blood-smeared boardwalk fronting Mahooney's bar. . . .

One more measure, and why not? Something to settle him, get them snake eyes off his back, douse his thinking against the images, the town, its folk, Hendy and his twisted interpretation of what stood for law and order. One more measure. The whole bottle if need be!

He thudded the bottle back to the table, finished the full-measured drink, and moved to the door, his grip on the knob wet and sticky. Bar would be dark and deserted now, Beanstalk long since taken to his bed, but he would have left his pail, mop and besom in readiness for the morning sweep through. Well, that would do fine, just fine; take no more than an hour at most to have another scrub at the blood-stains. Only decent thing to do. Damn it, this was his bar, his business; any proprietor worth his standing would want to keep his place clean – specially in a place as stained as Peaceway.

Take his mind off them snakes eyes while he was at it.

They were still there, like the stains, thought Mahooney, a half-hour later as he eased back on his knees and stared at the water-soaked floorboards. Stains might never shift, but the eyes had; moved along of him from the backroom to the wings, slid through the shadows, staring, waiting. There right now. Somewhere.

He shuffled back again, the slopped water trailing to his knees like a slithering snake. Leave it, he figured. Tell Beanstalk to put some real effort into his scrubbing in future. Meantime, just forget it. This was no time for the owner of Mahooney's bar to be seen scrubbing his own floors. Never live it down if somebody happened to be watching.

But somebody was, and a whole lot closer now. Somebody in the shadows, corner table, drawing slow and relaxed on a freshly lit cheroot. He could smell the drift of smoke.

'Blood on yuh boards same as blood on yuh hands, ain't it?'

The voice was as slow and easy as the curl of smoke, the words murmured carefully, measured, no hurry, no rush.

'Who's there? Who's that?' croaked Mahooney, the slopped water creeping between his knees. 'What yuh want? And just what in hell do yuh think yuh doin'—'

'Whoa now, steady there, fella. Wouldn't be in yuh

interests right now to go rousin' folk, would it?'

'Just who the devil are yuh?' Mahooney's eyes narrowed to tight, squinting slits. 'Step clear of that shade, mister, and show y'self.'

'No, I think not. Don't see the need. What we're about don't need faces, 'ceptin' yours, o'course, and I'm seein' that clear enough.'

Mahooney shuffled at the cold seep of water to his groin.

'Easy there,' said the voice. 'Don't get to shiftin' none, mister. Makes me nervous. 'Sides, yuh ain't through there, are yuh? Blood ain't faded one mite.' Smoke curled again, thicker and slower. 'Don't reckon it will neither. Not ever. Not while yuh stay playin' this dirty game.'

A shower of playing cards scattered across the water at Mahooney's knees. 'What in hell's name . . .' he hissed, his eyes bulging, a trickle of saliva sliding from the corner of his mouth.

'Found these along of a whole supply yuh got there in yuh back room. So how long yuh been handin' out marked packs to yuh customers? Your idea or Hendy's? That scumbag sheriff put yuh up to it? But yuh went along of it, didn't yuh? Happy enough, weren't yuh, to let strangers in town deal from a fixed deck – just like yuh did for that fella Brown t'night. How many times yuh set that trap so's Hendy can have his entertainment, keep the town sweet on a helpin' of lynch law, prove himself the big fella runnin' the show? How many times, Mahooney? Or yuh lost count?'

Mahooney shivered, sweated, swallowed on a parched throat, the seeping chill, and stared openmouthed at the sodden cards.

'Bet yuh got a whole heap of ruses up yuh mangy sleeves, eh?' droned the voice. 'Faked horse-thievin' among 'em? Sure it is.'

'Who are yuh, f'Cris'sake?' groaned Mahooney again, the sweat glistening on his brow.

'All the voices in the night yuh ever heard, Mahooney. Yuh recall them, don't yuh? Nights when yuh couldn't sleep 'cus of what yuh were hearin' – Hendy's orders, liquored mob at the hangin' tree out there, pleadin' of some innocent fella before the noose tightened. Sure, you recall 'em. Hearin' 'em now, ain't yuh?'

'Weren't just me,' stammered Mahooney, the water sloshing at his groin. 'There's others. Mac Ives down the livery, Clancy Springs, Joe Fane, Gus Smalley . . . whole town, damn it!' He choked on a swallow. 'Hendy's word's the law round here. There ain't no crossin' him. Never has been.'

' 'Cus nobody never tried. That's the sum of it, fella. Plain as that. Nobody raised so much as a spit. Till now.'

'Don't know who yuh are, mister, what yuh plannin',' gulped Mahooney, his hands shaking, jowls quivering, 'but yuh should know somethin' – somethin' to take count on: we got some big noise marshal due here matter of only hours, and I'm tellin' yuh—'

'I heard,' drawled the voice.

'Good, real good, 'cus there ain't goin' to be no place to hide for nobody come his steppin' in here.' Mahooney's eyes bulged brighter, rounder, the whites streaked with a mesh of bloodshot veins. 'Want my advice,' he croaked, easing slowly to his feet, 'yuh'd best get y'self clear. Right now. T'night, while yuh still got the time. Before Hendy and that marshal. . . .' He trembled. 'Hell, yuh got my oath on it, mister, shan't say a word to nobody about yuh bein' here, whoever yuh are. Not a word.'

'Yuh right, yuh won't – not one simperin' word,' said the voice, as the cheroot smoke curled, the shadow moved and the glint of a knife-blade shimmered in the soft night light.

Dubs Mahooney saw nothing of the joker from the scattered deck of cards floating at his boots.

THREE

'Pretty little thing, ain't yuh?' Sheriff Hendy sucked on the wad of chewing baccy, rolled it over his tongue and let his pointed index finger slide softly, slowly down the girl's cheek, into her neck and carefully on to the mound of her breasts. 'Yeah, real pretty,' he murmured, halting the finger, then pressing it harder until the girl flinched and backed to the edge of his cluttered desk.

'Half-breed, eh?' he grinned, relaxing the hand to his side. 'Ain't had me a 'breed before.' He sucked on the baccy, slanted his lips and aimed a line of spittle to a waiting can. 'Sioux, Apache, Comanche . . . which bit's which?' The grin slithered, hovered, faded to a sticky leer as his gaze darkened. 'Find out soon enough, eh?' The girl backed again, her eyes wide with fear.

'Yuh seein' this back there, Jameson?' called Hendy, without turning to the bruised, mottled face behind the cell bars. 'Yuh slaverin' over what yuh missin'? Well, yuh should be, fella, chance ain't never goin' to come your way again, is it? Nossir. Never goin' to have y'self a 'breed, are yuh? Nothin' of no kind, come to that.' He half-turned, his gaze narrowed. 'They're goin' to hang yuh out Utah way, Jameson. Did I mention that? No, well, they are – leastways, there's a marshal headin' out to claim yuh. Must be somebody, mustn't yuh, for a full-fledged, upstandin' marshal to bother with yuh, ride yuh on an iron horse all the way to Utah?'

The face behind the bars simply stared, unblinking, tight-lipped, silent in the shadowed gloom of the lantern-lit office.

'Shame about that,' said Hendy, one eye settling on the girl, ' 'cus I'll be frank, mister, I was lookin' forward to havin' the pleasure of seein' yuh squirm for m'self. Sure, I was. Opportunity of hangin' an all-time gunslinger right here in Peaceway don't come every day. That it don't. Shame. Still, I got that other scumbag penned along of yuh as compensation, ain't I? Mr-nobody-Brown. Fancy-coated marshal ain't goin' to be fussed none with him, is he? No chance. I figure for Mr Brown hangin' here, in *my* town.'

Hendy turned again, grabbed the girl and dragged her to him. The man behind the bars stayed staring, unblinking.

'Not normally in my nature to be generous to penned scum – *'specially* penned scum,' Hendy scowled. 'But seein' as how I gotta hangin' to spare, so to speak, and as how I'm goin' to stand good in the marshal's book 'cus of you, Jameson, I'm for dealin' yuh one last treat – sorta condemned man's breakfast.'

He reached to his desk for the bunch of jail keys, selected one and held it at eye-level to Jameson's face. 'Goin' to let yuh run yuh greasy fingers through the 'breed's hair, just so's yuh go to the noose with the memory – and the agony of what yuh know I'll be enjoyin'!'

Hendy's grin slithered cold and wet across his lips. 'Real friendly, ain't I?' he mouthed, unlocking the cell door and swinging it open. 'Generous to a fault! Now, get out here, damn yuh!'

The man hesitated, his tired, bruised gaze moving slowly from Hendy to the girl, beyond them to the office door, the window and the night-shadowed street.

'Don't get to no wild thinkin' there, fella,' said Hendy, pushing the girl to the desk again, laying aside the keys to run his fingers menacingly over the butt of his Colt. 'Yuh'd be one helluva bleedin' mess in two steps – and I ain't for havin' the place made untidy by the likes of you. Now, yuh taking up my offer or ain't yuh?'

Jameson ran his tongue over his lips, glanced quickly at the shivering, wet-eyed girl, the Colt drawn now and tight in Hendy's hand, and was turning, like a dazed figure in a drifting dream, when he flinched at Hendy's sudden sneer, the dance of shadows across the wall, and raised an arm instinctively against the lunge at his back.

The girl choked on a stifled scream, Hendy spat the baccy from his mouth and growled in the effort of the thudding whip of the Colt across the man's head, grabbed him as he crumpled, whipped him again, a third time, a fourth, again and again in a whirling flurry of lashings until the blood was flying, splattering the girl's face, the desk, the floor, and the man's lolling head was no more than a mass of broken flesh and matted hair.

'Ain't no smooth-talkin' marshal takin' my prison-

ers,' hissed Hendy, throwing the man to the floor.
'Nobody does that in my town! Yuh hear that, 'breed?
Yuh see that? Stood witness to it, didn't yuh? Fella
there tryin' to jump me?' The sweat gleamed like
moonlit ice on his face. 'Well, he ain't goin' no place
now, is he, save a hole up there on Boot Hill. Just
that!'

Hendy ran the barrel of the Colt across the palm
of his hand and stared at the smear of blood.
'Could've saved that dude marshal a whole journey,
couldn't I?' he drawled slowly, his eyes frozen in a
crazed focus. 'Ain't no need for no law here 'ceptin'
mine, is there? Yuh agree, 'breed? Sure yuh do. Yuh
tell that marshal good, eh, when he gets here? Tell
him how I stopped this sonofabitch from runnin'
wild in our town? My town!'

He turned to the cells. 'But don't you fret none,
Mr-sleepin'-nobody-Brown. You got the best to come.
A real live hangin' all to y'self!'

Hendy had turned again, holstered the Colt and
was reaching for the shivering girl when the sleeping
man in the shadows of the locked cell opened an eye
that seemed for a moment to pierce the sheriff's
back like a shaft of flame.

It had closed again when the girl began to moan.

Mac Ives was waiting like a gopher at its hole for that
waking wink of first light.

Hell, it was a time coming, he thought, his fingers
twisting nervously at the drooping curls of his mous-
tache. Livery here was still full of shadows and the
silence of night. Nothing moving, darn near a thing
breathing save for himself and the stabled horses.
Might almost be another world; some place where

living men slept deep and only the ghosts of them walked free.

Get to spooking himself with thoughts like that. Or maybe he already was: spooked deep to the gut so that not even a bottle of Mahooney's best – at a spooking price along of it! – was a cure for sleepless nights and grinding days and the hours of always looking back, wondering if the shadow following was your own or the shape of somebody sitting on your tail.

Well, all that was going to change, too right it was, minute the first light cleared that far horizon and he glimpsed the rider coming in.

Arrival of a full-fledged territorial marshal in Peaceway was probably going to be the town's last chance, last throw of the dice against Hendy and his paranoid rule of terror; perhaps the only chance anybody here would ever have to tell how it had come to be, how it was now and where it was all heading unless somebody – an authority big as a marshal, with a marshal's ways and maybe a marshal's guns – ended it, fast sure and forever.

You bet, just like that, this very day, thought Ives, shrugging his shoulders against the chill, before Hendy dragged another half-crazed soul to the hanging tree and the town stood witness once again to a lynching; stood right there, silent as the grave when it was done, and not a man among them without the blood of it all on his hands.

He grunted, shivered, and eased himself a step closer to the open doors and the still gloomy sprawl of empty lands to the trail twisting its way from Nape Sands. Marshal was certain to ride in from the Sands, he figured. Only decent trail hereabouts: straight as a barrel, fast and safe.

Hell, he thought, shivering again, just how many
fellows had ridden that trail, grateful for the sight of
a town, first hint of civilization in miles, with the
prospect of a beer, food, feather-bed maybe and the
time to settle the dust and dirt . . . and ended their
days stretched tight in a noose? How many? He had
lost count. Nobody was much for keeping a tab.

Only thought then had been how long before the
next clink and jangle of tack, soft pad of tired hoofs,
ease of old leather, sound of a stranger new to
town. . . .

'What's the goin' price on a dead man's horse?'

Ives swallowed, shivered, began to sweat, stared
through suddenly watering eyes, and turned without
hearing the scuff of his boots in the scattering of
straw to the voice at his back.

Nothing to see in the gloom back there. Nothing
moving, no shape, not so much as a stray shadow. His
mouth opened and stayed that way save for the hiss-
sodden, gulping groan.

'Hey, now,' clipped the voice lightly, 'horse-dealin'
fella like y'self lost for words? T'ain't natural. Yuh got
some touch of laryngitis there or somethin'?'

Ives gulped again and squinted, his arms loose,
feet leaden, the sweat cold at his neck.

'Know your trouble, fella? Business here's too
good. Gotten too steady and reg'lar. Yuh'd reckon
that? I'm readin' it right?'

The voice had shifted, a mite to the left there, into
the deeper gloom. Hell, where was the light? 'What
yuh want?' groaned Ives. 'Who the devil are yuh?'

'Been asked that more than once hereabouts.
Fella back there at the saloon had the same thing in
mind. . . . So I settled it for him. Sorta.'

'Yuh ain't. . . . Yuh ain't that marshal we're expectin', are yuh?' Ives took a step forward. 'Say, if yuh are,' he croaked, a nervous grin flickering at his lips, 'if yuh Marshal Quaid, I been waitin' on yuh. Right here. Most of the night.' He took another shuffled step. 'Didn't figure for yuh gettin' here till later. Reckoned as how yuh'd come through from the Sands, though. Best way. Wanted to be here to welcome yuh, tell yuh how it is. . . . Say, yuh don't have to stand there in the dark, mister. Ain't no need for that. Yuh step out now, let me get some coffee for yuh, eh? Bet yuh could use that. Sure yuh could. Me too! Hell, I tell yuh, Mr Quaid, this town ain't no place right now for a fella with any sorta delicate gut!'

Ives halted, feet leaden again, the sweat thicker and colder. 'Yuh still there, mister? Yuh hearin' me?' he rasped.

Silence. Nothing, save the low snort of a mount, softest shift of a hoof.

'Mister?' he croaked, squinting tight. 'Yuh there?' He swallowed. 'Don't have to show y'self, o'course,' he spluttered on. 'Hell, no. I mean, I know how you law fellas work. Sure I do. Seen 'em before, and 'specially when yuh hit a town like this.' He paused, licking at his lips. 'Guess yuh know about that, eh? About Hendy, way he runs this place, way he's got us all tied in. Some more so than others, o'course. Me – well, I just sorta fix the horses. Me and Clancy back there on the Sands. But I ain't never killed nobody. Nossir, not one. Just the horse fixin'. Swearin' to some fella ownin' a stolen mount. Nothin—'

'Turn 'em loose,' snapped the voice from the shadows.

'What?' groaned Ives.

'Yuh heard. Turn 'em loose. Every last horse yuh got here.'

'Mister, I couldn't—'

'Yuh got three minutes. Long as it takes to get this cheroot here glowin' steady enough to torch the place.' A curl of smoke drifted from the gloom. 'Three minutes.'

FOUR

Joe Fane ran his fingers slowly, rhythmically over the shredded strands of his loose braces, hitched his drooping pants and shuffled deeper into the shadows back of the ramshackle lean-to at Jessom's mercantile.

He was chilled through, gut-twisted nervous and seeing ghosts.

There were shapes and sounds about Peaceway that should not be there. Things he could not figure, that had never been there before, had no good reason to be here now and, worse, seemed in no hurry to leave.

Take Mahooney's bar for an instance. Light there at the back had not dimmed one mite through the night, not since the boys had finished cleaning up that fellow, Brown, delivered him to Hendy, along of the 'breed girl, and gone their ways. So what had kept Dubs so engrossed he had foregone his bed for a night in his back room? Darn sight more than a bottle of his best and the attentions of Lacy Alice.

And another thing, what in hell's name had been that noise at the batwings? A soft scrubbing sound, like somebody was doing just that – scrubbing the floorboards. Day Beanstalk got to being that particular would be enough to turn a fellow teetotal. But more to the point, why had the scrubbing stopped just as suddenly as it had started? Why was the back light still burning this close to sun-up?

And how come, he would swear on the Good Book, that something, somebody, had slipped away from the bar minute the scrubbing sound had died?

Seen it, or him, for himself, standing on the boardwalk there, no mistaking a definite shape, some fellow bent low and moving at a pace from the bar to Mac Ives' livery. Now just who in Peaceway would be doing that, middle of the night, without somebody knowing to it?

Unless, of course, there were folk about town that *nobody* knew to.

Supposing one of Jameson's scum partners was here to spring him; or supposing that nobody-fellow Brown had not been riding alone. No telling, not in a place like Peaceway with a sheriff like Hendy running it the way he did. Reputations spread fast, even out here.

So why not summon the courage and go see just what was happening, or had happened, at Mahooney's? Why not stop the skulking back here of the lean-to like some hound feared of a whipping for its nosiness and step out to the street, go stir Gus Smalley, Mac Ives, Hendy himself, damn it, and get this day started like any other?

No, not like any other. Today would see the arrival of that big-time marshal, Quaid. Today was going to be different; time dragging, folk fidgeting, watching, waiting on the night train.

You want to do something really useful, thought

Joe, hitching his pants again, why not go check with Sam Wards at the railhead that the train would be running to time? Only thing this town wanted was for Quaid and his prisoner to be aboard it – and no bones rattling back of him and no ghosts left to haunt.

He grunted, scratched his ginger stubble and was three steps to the street when the light broke fierce and bright to the east and the first flame licked out of the livery like a raging tongue.

Lacy Alice uncurled herself from the twist of sheets on the bed in her room above Mahooney's bar, brushed the tumble of hair from her face and stumbled to the window overlooking the street.

She blinked, once, twice, rubbed her eyes, wiped a hand over the night-sticky sweat at her neck and stared at the scurrying, dusty chaos below her.

'Sonofabitch,' she murmured, blinking again, 'what the hell's goin' on?'

Joe Fane running back and forth, shouting, yelling, waving his arms in a lather fit to drown him. Gus Smalley there, staggering out of the shadows, still pulling up his pants, his open shirt slapping at the mound of his gut like a full tide over rocks, rolling back in a daze as the billowing smoke began to sweep down the street. 'Fire! Fire!' he growled, loosing his grip on the pants as they slid to his ankles.

'The livery's goin' up!' shouted a man running from Amy Fisher's rooming-house, three others following, their eyes wide on the leaping flames, then clouded in the rush of smoke.

'Where the hell's Mac?'

'Somebody get to the horses, f'Cris'sake!'

'Ain't doin' no good just starin'!'

'How'd it get started?'

'What the hell – who cares? It's here. Do somethin'!'

'Don't let it spread!'

'Whole town could go up!'

The voices came thick and fast; bodies scurried, staggered, tumbled through still waking limbs; eyes blinked, stared; mouths opened and closed on the surging smoke.

Street was filling now, folk spilling from all corners, heading for the livery, yelling for water, pails. A man tripped and sprawled in the dirt; another jumped him, slopping the better part of a half-bottle of whiskey clutched in his hand; a woman gathered her skirts to her knees and stood screaming; two dogs began to fight, a cock screeched.

'Where's Hendy? Somebody go get the sheriff. . . .'

And with any luck at all, thought Alice, her lips twitching on a cynical grin, he might just get to being roasted alive!

Bart Jessom thundering out of his store now like a man possessed, his face grey as a secondhand funeral shroud. 'I been robbed,' he screamed. 'Somebody's raided the store!'

Nobody answered him, gave so much as a damn, and left him to rant right there on the boardwalk.

Alice had half-turned to reach into the jumble of discarded clothes for her dress, when Beanstalk slithered from the bar to the street his raised hands blood-smeared and shaking.

'Mahooney's dead!' he shuddered in his high-pitched, cackling voice. 'His throat's been slit! Yuh hear that? Mahooney's dead, right there, in the bar! Damn it, anybody listenin', f'Cris'sake?'

Alice stepped back from the window, shivered, clutched at the dress and gulped on a long, cold sigh. Livery burning, Mahooney dead, store robbed, and now Hendy barking his orders to the town.

'Get to that fire, damn yuh,' he screeched. 'All of yuh – every man here. Don't give a cuss about yuh store, Jessom. You – Beanstalk – go sort that bar. Dump Mahooney some place. Get this town cleaned up. I want it lookin' as it should come noon. Yuh hear? Do it, damn yuh, before I get to loosenin' somebody's gut with this piece! Now do it! Do it!'

Alice shivered again, fumbled into her dress, her fingers suddenly thick and heavy at the buttons, her hair tumbling across her face, the noise and panic from the street thudding in her head. Town was going mad, cartwheeling into chaos. Who had started the fire; who had slit Mahooney's throat? Hendy was spinning into a crazed mess, his town running out of control before his eyes. How, why, whose was the hand on the blade, behind the flame?

She tossed her hair into her neck, grabbed a ribbon and tied it back as she moved to the window again. Dust swirling under the rush of boots, shouts echoing, voices jumbled to a pitching mass at the livery; smoke clamouring high and thick, flames twisting through it, burning across the early light, shimmering against the first of the sun.

Town might soon be a furnace, she thought, turning back to the room, her gaze moving rapidly over the scattering of her belongings. Time to get clear, but nothing here worth saving – too many bad memories, tainted and stained with the dirt of

Peaceway, Mahooney, Hendy. No, nothing. Leave it, let it burn!

She shuddered at the sudden pounding on the door. 'Alice, Alice – yuh gotta get out, now!'

The bar girls jostling in the corridor, one of them crying, another sobbing deep and pitiful.

'Get y'selves out, yuh hear?' she called. 'Don't wait. Just go. Anyway yuh choose. Just go!'

Back stairs to the alley, she thought, the sweat trickling at her neck. Get to Hendy's office, the 'breed girl – what was left of her – and then maybe, yes, one of the mounts always hitched there. If she moved fast, no hesitating, no stopping to think too long on it, and no looking back, not for nothing, she might get clear.

Grab the girl, snaffle a mount, and just ride – to the north, the way station out at Trail Ridge. Stage passed through there once a week. Keep going, anywhere, anyhow. Damn – no money! Did it matter? Been living on her natural 'assets' for years. Too late now to ponder the morals of it.

So move, put this town behind you while the chance was there and leave the rest to the hell of its own making!

Alice had reached the door, opened it and was one step into the corridor when the shattering roar of an explosion blew the window into the room, showering glass and splinters of timber like needles of rain and tossing her against the wall in a swirling flash of skirts.

Last thing she heard before passing out was a crazed fellow shouting down there in the street that somebody had blown up the hanging tree.

FIVE

The cell door rattled in the thrust of the blast and the man behind it was a long half-minute before he dared to open his eyes.

The lantern glow had dimmed and the flame died in the rush of the draught, the curled, stained papers on Sheriff Hendy's desk scattered to the floor, an unwashed tin plate skidded and come to rest balanced above a hanging drawer, an empty bottle crashed against a chair leg and cracked, and the dust of a place not cleaned in months drifted like a mizzle in the shafts of light from the window.

The half-breed girl had not moved from her hide in the darkened corner; simply winced and blinked and pulled the rags of her clothes across her body.

'What the hell—' mouthed the man, swallowing and tightening his grip on the bars. He licked his lips and turned his gaze on the girl. 'The keys,' he hissed. 'Get 'em. One of the drawers – to yuh right.'

The girl nodded, struggled to her feet and padded barefoot to the desk, glancing fearfully at the battered body of Jameson in the second cell, murmuring softly to herself as she opened a drawer and rummaged among its rubbish.

'The one in the middle. Try that,' hissed the man again.

The girl moved on, dragged at the middle drawer, groaning as it held tight, pulled again and stepped back sharply on the clattering spill of its contents to the floor.

'Yuh got 'em?' croaked the man, his knuckles whitening under the pressure of his grip.

The girl was on her knees, still rummaging, scattering useless bits and pieces, when the door to the office crashed open and a figure, tall, sweating, dirt-streaked and breathing heavily filled the space.

'Not a sound,' he whispered, closing the door softly behind him, pausing a moment to blink, catch on the heaving breath, glance quickly to the cell and then, with the sliding wipe of a hand across his face, ease back against the door and shake his head through a long sigh.

'One helluva way to start a day!' he grinned, his eyes gleaming through the sparkle of sweat.

The girl had shuffled from the desk to the shadows, her face tight again with terror, her fingers shaking over the rags at her breasts; the man behind the bars simply stared, a nerve twitching at his temple.

'Sorry I didn't make it sooner,' said the man, relaxing on another blink, a quick lick of his lips. 'Had a busy night, and seems like I've raised' – he crossed softly to the window, fingered the dust from a pane and peered through it – 'somethin' of a stir out there.' He turned, easing aside the folds of his dust-coat on a holstered Colt and sheathed knife. 'Name's Friar – Morgan Friar. Pleased to meet yuh. Brown, ain't it?'

The man at the bars swallowed. 'S'right, but how come—'

'All in good time, fella, all in good time. Shan't ask yuh what happened to Jameson. Can see for m'self. That him in the cell next to yuh? Hendy's doin'? Figures. But right now—'

He swung back to the window at the sound of shouts and yells as the street began to fill with a running mob of men.

'Gettin' too close,' he murmured, squinting. 'Time we weren't here.'

'Hang on there, mister,' began Brown again.

'Not here, not now,' snapped Friar, stepping from the window to the desk, 'Mornin', ma'am,' he smiled at the kneeling, shivering girl. 'No cause for alarm there, but I'd be grateful if yuh'd hand up them keys so's we can all three of us move on some.'

The girl's hand slid back to the scattered bits, rummaged, settled and lifted the bunch of cell keys.

'That's fine, ma'am, just fine. Shall we go?'

It took just three minutes then for Brown to be standing free, the girl at his side, and for Morgan Friar to be beckoning them to the open back door to the alley beyond.

'Stay tight, stay close, and just follow me. All right?' He lifted the bunch of keys, grinned and pocketed them. 'Might come in useful, eh?'

They disappeared into the smoke-filled town as silently as ghosts.

'Somebody's goin' to hang,' growled Hendy, slapping a wad of chewing baccy round his mouth as he paced slowly round the shattered remains of the hanging tree and the blackened, tangled mass of torn roots at its crater. 'Yuh hear me there? Somebody's goin' to hang.'

'*Somebody*'s been doin' a whole lot around town,' grunted Joe Fane, tugging on his braces. 'A whole sight too much to my likin', and I wanna know—'

'We got trouble,' spat a man at the back of the gathering. 'I can smell it. Mahooney, the livery, now this. . . . What the hell's happenin' here? Anybody tell me, f'Cris'sake?'

'Ives said as how he reckoned for it bein' that marshal we're expectin',' chipped a lounging youth. 'Never seen him full on, but figures it for him all the same.'

'Ives got that fire out yet?' drawled Hendy, still pacing.

'It's out,' sighed Fane, rubbing a hand across his brow. 'Livery ain't worth a spit, and there ain't a lick of horse flesh to be seen, but flames didn't spread none – thank the Lord.'

Hendy halted, floated a long fount of brackish spittle to the dirt and turned his gaze to the gathering, the littered street, the silent, watchful faces at smoke-misted windows, then, without warning, spun on his heel to grab at Bart Jessom's shirt and haul him close.

'Should've had that dynamite locked away safe, shouldn't yuh?' he mouthed, screwing the handful of shirt to a ball in his hand. 'This wouldn't have happened then, would it, yuh mule-head? Pity whoever did this didn't blow yuh damn store first!' He threw the storekeeper to the ground. 'So who took the stuff? Yuh see anybody?'

'Never saw a soul, Mr Hendy, not a livin' thing,' spluttered Jessom. 'Swear to it.'

Hendy spat again and turned back to the mob. 'Now listen up there, all of yuh,' he scowled. 'What's happened here ain't the work of no law-keepin' marshal – don't make no sense for it to be so.' He rolled the wad of baccy through another slapping chew. 'Marshal Quaid ain't here yet, right? Yuh got my word on it. So, who we got skulkin' round town – *my* town – with a mind crazed enough to go blowin' and torchin' the place apart and gettin' blade-happy with it? Any ideas? Any one of yuh got a notion?'

'Hell, Mr Hendy, ain't none of us for doin' nothin' like that,' called a man. 'What we wanna do that for?'

'I'll tell yuh what we got,' said Joe Fane, gripping his braces. 'I seen him.'

The gathering stared and murmured. 'What yuh see, Joe?' asked the lounging youth.

Fane took a step forward, glanced quickly at Hendy, then turned to the waiting faces. 'Ain't been sleepin' so good these nights,' he began, relaxing the braces. 'Get to bein' about all hours.'

'Don't sleep so good m'self,' croaked an old-timer, 'but I ain't seen nobody. Don't see so good neither!'

'Spit it out, Joe,' snapped Jessom, coming slowly to his feet. 'Yuh seen somethin', we gotta know. Hell, we go on like this—'

'I heard somebody back there at Mahooney's,' said Fane, stretching his braces, beginning to sweat. 'And he weren't no late drinker neither. And then I seen him, not close, just scuttlin' away – to the livery! Not one of us, vouch for that, nobody I recognized, but supposin'—'

'No supposin'.' growled Hendy. 'We ain't here for supposin'. Yuh get back to doin', all of yuh. Find this fella, yuh hear? And yuh don't stop lookin till yuh turned every last speck of dirt.' He spat the wad of baccy to the ground. 'Ain't nobody gets to messin' with my town. Nobody!'

'What if—' began the lounging youth.

'No "what ifs", "supposin's", nothin'.' Hendy's glare darkened across the mob. 'We got just a few short hours till that marshal—'

'Yuh seen this?' shouted Beanstalk from the far end of the street. 'Yuh'd sure as hell better! I seen it, with my own eyes. Sure I have.' He wrapped his hands in his apron as he shuffled slowly to the mob. 'Yuh ain't got no prisoners no more, Mr Hendy. Not livin' anyhow. Jameson's dead, right there in the cell, and that other fella – he's gone!'

Hendy's glare seemed suddenly lost in the grey of his pallor and the twitch at his lips.

SIX

Lacy Alice stared deep into the cracked mirror propped on the splintered remains of her dressing-table and dabbed carefully at the blood smears from the cuts on her face.

She looked a wreck, she thought, stood here with her hair straggling like wet straw across her shoulders, the skin stained and bruised, dress heaped around her in torn folds, brown eyes bulging and red-rimmed as a frenzied heifer's, lips cracked and still trembling. Felt it too – and smelled like a scorched strip of old rag.

'Hell!' she mouthed, and dabbed again, one eye on the mirror, the other flicking anxiously to the hole in the wall where there had once been a window.

Street was a deal quieter now; only the occasional shout, curse, sound of hurrying steps, distant crash of timbers from the livery. Fire seemed to be under control, but the smell of drifting smoke, the acrid stench of the explosion, lingered deep in the already sun-high day.

No sound of Hendy's growls, not since he had ranted at the mob, then stood there in the street staring and suddenly silent at the approach of Beanstalk

37

from his office. Some news there for him to digest, she grinned, wincing at the sting of a cut. Dog's dinner to a stringy steak Hendy had killed Jameson – no 'prisoner' ever left his cells save to an execution on home soil but just who had released that soft spoken, well-dressed fellow, Brown?

Perhaps a deal more to the point, she grinned again, how was Sheriff Hendy going to explain *that* to the law-upholding Marshal Quaid when he hit town at noon?

Time for figuring was running out – a deal faster than she cared to reckon, she thought, throwing aside the blood-smeared pad, straightening her hair, pulling at the dress. Too late now to get to the girl, snaffle a mount and make it to the way station. The 'breed would have to look to herself along with the rest of the girls. But there was another possibility, another way of putting the misery of Peaceway behind her once and for all.

There was the night train to Utah.

She stepped carefully over the shattered glass to the leaning door, paused, looked tentatively to left and right along the smoke-misted corridor, and waited, listening.

Any amount of raised voices down there in the bar; men sating their thirsts between bouts of 'telling it' the way they had seen it, each with a theory as to how the chaos, mayhem and murder of that day had started, and just where it might be heading.

'We should've seen it comin'. Can't run a town accordin' to Hendy's law and stay clean. T'ain't possible.'

'Hendy hear yuh talkin' like that and you're a dead man.'

'What we're all thinkin' though.'

'I'll tell yuh what *I'm* thinkin' – what the lot of yuh should be thinkin' yuh got two bits of sense. I'm thinkin' as to how it is some fella can slip round this town like a rat, slit Mahooney's throat, torch the livery, blow the hangin' tree to kingdom come and open up that cell easy as pickin' candy from a jar, and nobody – but nobody – knows who in hell he is, where he's come from, why he's here, or just who or what among us is goin' to be next. *That*'s what I'm thinkin'.'

'I'm thinkin' about that marshal due here noon.'

'If there is a marshal due here noon.'

'And what's that supposed to mean, f'Cris'sake?'

'How the hell should I know? I'm just thinkin' it.'

A hushed, thoughtful silence; scrape of a boot, shift of a bottle. Somebody cleared his throat, another belched. Creak of the batwings. A new arrival.

Alice wiped the sweat from her neck and eased along the corridor to the shadows at the head of the stairs and peered into the crowded bar below.

'I'm all through, washed up,' croaked Mac Ives, dragging himself to the bar, his face a smoke and dirt-smeared, wrinkled mass, lips cracked and pinched, eyes wide, grey as wet snow and bloodshot. 'Ain't a stick of that livery standin' worth a spit. No stock neither.'

He slumped back, groaned, then settled his stare as if into nowhere. 'I'm pullin' out,' he croaked again to the silent, watching faces, 'Nothin' else for it. Get m'self outa this hell before it gets me. Yuh hear? Yuh listenin' to me there?'

'Sure we are,' said a man softly, easing the sweat at

the band of his hat. 'Ain't nobody here could blame yuh, Mac, but—'

'Yuh see who did it?' snapped a man at the window. 'Yuh see his face.'

'No, never did,' murmured Ives, 'but I sure as hell heard him. I heard his voice plain enough. Oh, yes, I heard that, every word. . . . His stare widened. 'Know somethin'? I heard a killer speakin' back there. A real, live, sonofabitch killer. That's what we got stalkin' this town. A killer – deadly as they come.'

Alice shivered, the sweat in her neck trickling cold and clinging. No point in listening to more of this, she thought, sweeping the torn dress across her feet. Just get out, now, before. . . .

Another creak at the batwings, thud of a firmer step.

'There'll be no pullin' out,' growled Hendy, straddling the doorway like some perching crow. 'Nobody leaves. Nobody.'

He chewed slowly on a wad of baccy, his lips spreading to a thin grin. 'Jameson tried that, and yuh all seen what happened to him, ain't yuh? Well, ain't yuh?'

Hendy's stare moved from silent face to silent, watchful face. 'Brown got lucky – for now. Don't figure for it rubbin' off on any of you. All right? No pullin' out. I makin' m'self clear?'

'Not in my book yuh ain't,' said Ives, pushing himself from the bar. 'Nothin' like it. Only thing clear to me is how we got to this. That's clear enough.' His arms hung loose, the stare deepened and narrowed on Hendy. 'Law-abidin' town, eh? Oh, sure, that's what we all wanted. Law-abidin', decent place a fella could sleep easy, trust the shadows and the folk makin' 'em. But that's *real* law, ain't it, Hendy? Somethin' yuh wouldn't know about, 'cus your law is a hangin' every time a fella sets foot here. Your law is livin' off our backs and killin' when it suits or some soul gets to askin' how it is—'

The single shot was fierce, fast, a sudden, ripping blaze from the Colt at Hendy's hip that surged the blood at Mac Ives' gut before he had formed another word, that crumpled him to a silent, twisted heap and left the echo of the shot hanging in the air like a strangled moan.

'There'll be no more of that,' drawled Hendy, rolling the chewing baccy as he holstered the Colt. 'Clear enough now?' Nobody moved in the stifling silence. 'Good. So perhaps yuh'll shift yuh lazy butts and get to findin' that scumbag we got dirtyin' our street. Yuh got just two more hours. Yuh hear? Two hours till we present ourselves decent and law-abidin' to Marshal Quaid. Now shift!'

Boots scuffed, chairs scraped. A bottle rolled across the floor. Beanstalk's besom scratched eerily, but no one mouthed a word as they filed from the bar to the boardwalk and spilled like flotsam to the sunlit street.

Hendy waited, rolling the baccy behind his slanted grin, then turned and walked to the stairs to the bar's private rooms.

'Alice?' he called. 'Yuh up there? Yuh'd just better be. We got some talkin' to do.'

But the corridor was deserted and the shadows lifeless.

'Short straws,' hissed Joe Fane, hugging the shadow back of Jessom's store. 'We'll do it that way. Shortest drawn does it. Steps up there to Hendy and blasts him to oblivion. Ain't nothin' else for it. Yuh agree?'

The two men facing him murmured and shuffled their feet in the dirt. 'Sounds easy,' said the slimmest, hunching his shoulders. 'But when yuh come to it—'

'Damnit, we got any other choice?' snapped Fane. 'Ain't nobody goin' to have the guts to say a word to that Marshal Quaid, are they? And minute he's on that train t'night – hell, we'll be back where we were.'

'So what about that fella Ives said spoke like a killer? And what about that fella Brown? Where're they? Yuh got any notion? Could be they're still in town. Right now. Could be the fellas—'

'Hell, I'll do it m'self,' clipped Fane, pulling on his braces. 'Go get a piece and shoot Hendy wherever I find him. Sure I will. Sheriff's gone rantin' crazy, mad as a dog, and I ain't for standin' to that. No how. Not after Mac bein' gunned down like that. No sayin' who's goin' to be next.' He slid the braces tight to his shoulders. 'You fellas stand to me? Yuh'll do that? So let's do it. Right now, before that clock in Mahooney's bar strikes noon.'

SEVEN

Morgan Friar flicked open the cover to his timepiece, held the face to the shaft of light through the cobwebs at the gap in the wall of the tumbledown shack, peered at it for a moment and closed it again with a satisfied grunt.

'Goin' to time,' he murmured, settling the silver piece to his pocket as he eased back and stretched his legs across the dirt floor. He wiped a hand slowly over his dark, bristling stubble and fixed his gaze on the man watching him from the deepest of the shadows.

'Not much in the way of comforts,' he grinned, 'but a sight better than Hendy's cell, eh? Yuh reckon?'

'Sure,' croaked the man, 'a whole lot better, but I'd just like to know—'

Friar held a finger to his lips. 'Be as well to keep yuh voice down, Mr Brown,' he urged, holding the finger to the air. 'Don't want them townfolk scuttlin' this way. They're a mite tetchy right now. Could get to doin' anythin'. Understandably so, o'course. Given 'em good cause, ain't we?'

'Don't know so much about the "we",' said the man, wincing on the painful shift of his body. 'Seems

43

to me yuh been raisin' all the hell round here. What I'd like to know is—'

'All part of my plannin', Mr Brown. Preparin' the ground, yuh might say.'

'Sorry,' sighed Brown, 'I ain't followin' yuh.' He winced again and glanced at the girl huddled in the far corner. 'Yuh in on this, lady, or just trailin' along of it like m'self?'

The 'breed girl hugged the shreds of her dress to her and shook her head.

'Figured not,' said Brown. 'So that's two of us, mister – and we're all ears.'

Friar turned to the gap, brushed the cobwebs aside and squinted through the shaft of light. 'You're a gamblin' man, Mr Brown, ain't yuh? Reckoned that as soon as I clapped eyes on yuh in Mahooney's last night – before them fellas got to spoilin' with yuh. Must've gotten a whole lot down on yuh luck to drift into a place like Peaceway. Still, that's as mebbe. Fact is, yuh luck's changed. You bet it has.'

He swung away from the gap, a smile creasing the spread of stubble. 'Play yuh hand to my dealin' from here on, Mr Brown, and I'd say yuh'd struck it rich as it comes.'

'Yuh would?' sighed the man, leaning back, his gaze on the splintered roof boards. 'Well, yuh'd be right on one score: I ain't about to step out to one of Hendy's hangin' entertainments, that's for sure. And I'm grateful to yuh for that. But, to be frank, mister, I'd just as soon get m'self a horse some place – if yuh ain't already scattered the lot of 'em – and put Peaceway far back of me as possible.' He lowered his gaze and grinned softly. 'Yuh'll appreciate my feelings.'

'Sure I do,' grunted Friar. 'Who wouldn't after the sorta handlin' you had, but that wouldn't be takin' no account of the natural habits of a gamblin' man, not when there's a whole shipment of bank gold about to drop at his feet just waitin' to be picked up. And you are a gamblin' man, aren't yuh, Mr Brown? Saw that in the cut of yuh coat, tailored shirt, way yuh handled them cards. Spotted they were marked, didn't yuh? Sure yuh did.' He clicked his fingers and smiled. 'Listen, we ain't got that much time. There's a train due here t'night shippin' close on forty thousand dollars in gold to the Utah banks of Western Central – only it ain't goin' no place, not once it pulls into Peaceway. End of the line, yuh might say. For everybody.'

Brown swallowed slowly. 'I'm listenin',' he clipped.

'I got friends on board that train, mister, been keepin' a watch on its cargo since it was loaded at Gratton and the train pulled out two days back. Soon as it reaches Peaceway, they take it, calm as yuh like, no problem, 'cus I'll be runnin' the town by then. Mine! A coupla my boys I left back at the Sands helpin' themselves to wagons and teams'll be here to load the shipment, and then, my friend, Peaceway is dust and the world's our oyster.' He grinned. 'I still got yuh attention there?'

'I'm keepin' pace of yuh,' said Brown.

'I been here coupla days or so, holed up anywheres I wouldn't be noticed. Watchin' and waitin'. Heard all about Hendy and his style of law keepin'. Got this town spooked and runnin' in its own shadow. Suits me fine. T'ain't done yet, though, nothin' like. Priority is to settle with that two-bit sheriff and then some marshal due here noon. Town's gotta be mine come dusk, but I need a helpin' hand, mister, and I figure yuh for bein' my man.'

'Yuh do?' frowned Brown.

'Gamblin' fella don't never lose sight of the pot in my experience. Stays sharp till the game's done, plays it hard and shrewd – and he ain't never for throwin' down a skinny hand.' Friar's eyes gleamed again behind the soft grin. 'That right?'

Brown shrugged. 'Yuh got the gun there, ain't yuh?'

'See, I was right! Gamblin' man always figures the odds.' Friar's grin slid away. 'Fair share of the gold for yuh standin' to me till that train pulls in – we gotta a deal? Yuh owe me.'

'Well,' drawled Brown, shifting with a wince, 'let's see now. . . .'

'Don't take too long chewin' on it. I'm a busy man.'

'Like I say, grateful yuh sprung me, but yuh still got the gun, so I figure if I don't stand to yuh, knowin' what I know, I'm a dead man anyhow. Put like that, the odds stack awful high.'

'That's my man,' grinned Friar. 'Knew it last night.'

'Well, mebbe yuh did – but just who are you, mister?' frowned Brown. 'If I'm hooked into this "situation" yuh got here, might be useful if I had a proper introduction to the fella I'm standin' to.'

'Me?' said Friar. 'Yuh don't really wanna know, do yuh? Don't count for none, does it? So let's just say I'm a man lookin' for an easier life than's been dealt me this far. And I'm seein' it comin' in on that night train.' His gaze tightened. 'At any price, mister. *Any* price. Just keep it in mind, eh?'

'Sure,' murmured Brown. 'Made that clear

enough already, ain't yuh?' He shifted painfully. 'What about the girl there? She ain't deaf, yuh know.'

'She's yours,' drawled Friar. 'On account. Only don't let her loose. All right? She steps outa line, I'll kill her.' He came to his feet and patted the butt of his Colt. 'There's a Winchester back of yuh. Grab it and let's go take ourselves a town, shall we?'

'The rail head,' whispered Lacy Alice to herself as she slipped into the cover and shadows of the stacked crates and barrels at the back of Mahooney's bar. The only place, only chance.

She shivered at the sound of a door being flung open, scrape and thud of a boot; the cracked, hissing snap of Hendy's voice.

'Alice, damn yuh. Yuh out here?'

She swallowed, slow and dry, felt the sweat cold on her cheeks, trickling to her neck, her fingers tight on the rough edge of a crate, closed her eyes and prayed.

'Alice?'

Hendy took a step forward, cursing softly, his jaw working anxiously on a wad of baccy, gaze narrowed and dark. 'Damn yuh!' He spat, turned and thudded back to the door and the silence of Mahooney's back room.

Alice shivered again, opened her eyes and licked at the sweat. Wait, she thought. Do not move a muscle. Hendy was shrewd enough to step out for a second look. Give it a minute, maybe two, then hug the cover of the crates as far as the old shacks out there. Nobody put them to any good use these days; just dust, dirt, cobwebs and rotting timbers. Perfect place to hide till the town was quiet again and she could risk the scurry across open ground to the rail head. And once there. . . .

Well, Sam Wards owed her sure enough. Did he just! His unpaid 'account' to her stretched as far back as the line he watched from that freight and telegraph office he never left. Fair trade, she reckoned, for a ticket and a safe seat deep into Utah.

She eased herself higher in the crates, gazed at the closed door, bit at her lip and slid on to the next shadow. Pause, listen. No hint of Hendy now. All quiet. She swung her gaze to the shacks, a half-dozen of them crouched there like worn bodies in stiff capes. Any one of them would suit, but maybe the leaning heap nearest the cattle pens.

She moved again, softly, almost on the tips of her button boots. Another crate, another shadow, and another trickling of the cold sweat. Pause, watch. She could make it to the first shack if she could summon the nerve. All she had to do. . . .

A creak of timber out there, a shadow, growing, stretching over the dirt from the far shack. Hell, there was somebody already there; somebody leaving more like, real careful, slow and soft as a bird.

Alice sank into the cover, her gaze fixed on the shadow, watching its reach; thickening now and spreading. Damn it, more than one body! She sank lower, hands flat and hot on a crate as the shadow reached again, took on a shape and then a face.

Morgan Friar! She swallowed and stifled a shiver. Friar – about the last person she had ever expected to see in a place like Peaceway; the one person she had never wanted to see here or anywhere else come to that. And just about the very last person this town would ever want to see again.

She squirmed at the sting of the chill at her spine. Morgan Friar haunting the streets sure as hell explained a lot of what had happened in the past few hours, and raised a still uglier prospect.

Last time she had seen the gunslinging hell-raiser he had been drunk on cheap whiskey in Beaver Falls out Nebraska way. But not too drunk to be renewing his vow loud and clear to be waiting on the day to settle a long time score. 'Bullet or blade, don't matter. I ain't fussed,' he had growled.

Target of his hatred then had been the same as it would be now. A certain no messing, law-punching marshal.

Name of Quaid.

EIGHT

Joe Fane had got himself a gun. An old piece, worn, but not used, 'not serious, anyhow, since way back,' Bart Jessom had explained. 'Day that kid from Colorado took out Shotts Cutler right there in the street. Yuh remember that? Well, this is the piece Shotts was still clutchin' when he hit the dirt. What yuh want it for?'

Joe had been careful not to say precisely what he had in mind, only that, with the town jumping like it was and there being somebody about with no real regard for who he might settle on next, a fellow felt a whole lot safer with a gun at his belt.

'Know how yuh feel,' Bart had grunted. 'Ain't nobody feelin' anythin' like safe no more. Tough sheriff and a clean town's one thing, but now. . . . Hell, Hendy's gotten it outa hand.'

'Maybe we all have,' Joe had wanted to say, but thought better of it. Loose talk could spread awful fast, especially over the counter of the only store in town with Bart Jessom behind it.

'Say this, though,' Bart had murmured, moving closer as he spun the chamber of the gun, 'that marshal we got visitin' ain't goin' to be impressed

50

none if Hendy's still buzzin' like a bee in a pot and
that fella Brown and whoever sprung him's still loose.
And he ain't going to be none too happy neither at
havin' no prisoner with him when he climbs aboard
that train. Strikes me best thing Hendy could do is
make himself real scarce. What yuh reckon?'

But Joe had offered neither comment nor opinion. He had simply paid for the gun, slid it to the
pocket of his loose trousers, hitched his braces and
left.

'Yuh go easy with that piece, yuh hear?' Bart had
called. 'Don't go makin' a Shotts Cutler of y'self.
T'ain't worth it.'

But this time there would be no stand-off in the
middle of the street, not the way Joe was planning it.
This time Shotts' old Colt would be the only piece
blazing. Two bullets. Two minutes to noon.

Gus Smalley had his priorities – first of them being to
stay alive in a town at a time when death was getting
to be awful common and a sight too regular; second
being to grab himself a share of the spoils while the
going offered it.

And Mahooney's bar had been up for grabs
minute that blade had slid across Dubs' throat.

Somebody had to step into his shoes, Gus had
figured. Town, whatever its state – and more so state
Peaceway was in right now – was no town at all without a bar, some place for a fella to cool off, stay sane,
have himself some time outside the shadows.

Gus had not waited to reckon it a deal further and
been the first to get Mahooney's cleaned up, organized and open to the town as usual. Even managed
to get the handful of girls back to something like

business. But not Lacy Alice. Nossir, not her, damn it, he thought, scuffing his boots through the broken glass on the floor of her room.

Alice had disappeared, just vanished like she was no more than a flicker of last light before a storm. He crunched to the hole that had once been a window overlooking the brooding, silent street. No telling where she might be; somewhere in town perhaps, or maybe she had taken off, ridden out for almost anywhere. Hell, she had been threatening to do just that for long enough.

But he needed her, needed her bad if he was going to lay anything like a permanent claim to Mahooney's bar. Alice was the only one in town able to handle Hendy, or at least keep him one step short of total madness.

And he was no more than a splice of boot leather short of that right now – right there in the bar, a bottle on the table in front of him, his back to the wall, gleaming Colt to hand, wad of baccy squelching round his mouth, and a look in his eyes that said all there was to say about what was going through his mind.

Nobody had a need to look twice.

Gus grunted, turned and crunched back to the door. No point in just hoping for Alice to show herself again, time had come to go look for her. Try the rooming-house, funeral parlour, Doc's place, old shacks back of the rail head. He paused, scratching slowly at his belly. Rail head itself, come to that.

If Alice had a real mind to put Peaceway behind her, night train to Utah might be the perfect means, specially bearing in mind Sam Wards' soft spot for her. Ticket to anywhere would be an easy price for him to pay for an hour or so of Alice's time.

Sure, thought Gus, heading for the stairs to the bar, the railhead; should have figured it sooner. Get himself out there right now, before that Marshal Quaid hit town, and before, more to the point, whoever it was tearing the place apart got to his next trick.

Or Hendy decided to ease himself clear of that table and go looking for it.

Gus had turned again, reckoning it being a deal more discreet to slip out the back way, when the swing and creak of the batwings had halted him and brought him on slow, soft steps to the stair-head.

Now just what was it lathering Joe Fane down there to a state where he looked as if he would either drop where he stood or rant like a tethered bull? Worked himself to some sweat and his hands were none too steady neither. He been hitting some private bottle, seen something he would sooner not have? Or was it. . . ?

Hell, he was carrying a gun, right there in his trouser pocket; could see the bulge of it, the weight dragging on his braces. Joe was no fellow for arming himself, never had been. Always figured for a toted piece being a one-way ride to Boot Hill.

He was moving now, careful, measured steps towards Hendy. Sheriff was not for taking a deal of notice. Why should he? Joe had always stood to Hendy, right from the start; he was a trusted man, one of the boys. Damn it, Joe Fane had noosed a rope more times than. . . .

'Sonofabitch!' hissed Gus, stepping quickly, heavily to the stairs, his gaze clamped like a leech on the shaking, twitching drift of Joe's hand to the trouser

pocket. That fool, baggy pants fellow was all for drawing his piece on Hendy! He was going to blast him,
point blank, the barrel close as a breath to the sheriff's face.

'Hey, Joe,' called Gus, thudding down the stairs.
'Just the fella. Wanted a word there.'

Joe trembled to a shuffling halt, arms loose at his
sides, the sweat glistening on his face, eyes wide and
bulging. His mouth dropped open before he gulped
on a surge of saliva.

Hendy poured himself another drink, sank it and
eased back in the chair, hands behind his head, a
levelled, cynical grin at his lips. 'Don't let me interrupt nothin' here,' he murmured. 'Or was it me yuh
wanted to see, Joe?', He glanced at the bar clock.
'Comin' up noon. Yuh see anythin' of that marshal
yet? Found the fella stalkin' us?' His hands broke free
of his head and flattened on the table to within a
finger of the Colt. 'What yuh been doin', Joe?
Somethin' useful, I hope.'

'Ain't we all?' blustered Gus, stepping quickly to
the bar, putting himself between Joe and Hendy, one
eye flicking anxiously to the bulge in Fane's pocket.
'Ain't a man of us not been busy, but fact is—'

'Joe gotta tongue in his head, ain't he?' drawled
Hendy, his fingers drumming lightly on the table. 'So
what's the news, eh? That stalker still on the loose?
Hell, t'ain't that big a town, is it? How many hidin'
places we got? How many does a fella *need*,
f'Cris'sake?' He hoisted himself slowly to his feet, one
hand coming to rest on the butt of the Colt. 'Yuh
sure yuh been lookin' close enough, Joe?'

Fane gulped again, blinked and wiped the sweat
from his face. 'Sure, we have,' he croaked. 'Ain't

nowhere we ain't turned over – and more than once. Just about every place yuh can think of.'

'Every place, Joe?' sneered Hendy. 'Well, now, I somehow doubt that.'

'He's right,' said Gus. 'I seen 'em. Fellas every-where. Seems like that sonofabitch's just vanished. Or mebbe he's left town, eh? Pulled out, that fella Brown and the 'breed along of him. Hell, what's it matter, anyhow? Marshal don't know nothin' of this, does he? Mebbe he don't need to. Why don't we just get–'

'Why don't yuh shut yuh mouth, Gus?' snapped Hendy. He holstered the Colt and glanced at the clock. 'Two minutes to noon, Joe,' he grinned. 'So what yuh goin' to do now?'

Gus Smalley had a terrible, deep-gut feeling that he knew precisely what Joe Fane was going to do. He could see it in the fellow's eyes, suddenly cold and fixed in their stare, like a window to the churning fear that had calmed now in his mind; eyes that were seeing just one shape in that light-shafted, deserted bar where the only sound was the slow, rhythmic tick of the clock.

He could see it too in the shift of Joe's right hand to the trouser pocket, the twitchy flex of the fingers, the softest stiffening of one shoulder.

Hell, he was going to reach for that piece, drag it from his pocket like it was a half-ton weight, his fingers wet and sticky in a grip that would not be there when it counted most. And Hendy would have all the time in the world to see it, watch every last movement of the fumbled effort; time to roll that wad of baccy round his mouth, settle his stance, ease his gun hand just the fraction needed for it to flash to a draw Joe would never see, save when the Colt was levelled, steady and blazing and it was all too damned late.

'Well, Joe, yuh lost yuh tongue again?' drawled Hendy.

Gus was half into a step forward; Joe Fane's hand had moved; Hendy had stiffened; the clock had ticked to noon and its innards grated the first grind to chime the hour, when the blade thudded into the bar-room floor and shimmered there like a shard of sunlight.

'Easy as yuh go, fellas,' clipped the voice from somewhere on the shadowed stairs. 'Don't wanna get to scrubbin' the place down again, do we?'

NINE

Morgan Friar descended the stairs to the bar like a man with nothing more on his mind than having himself a quiet drink. He came easy, step at a time, no hurry, relaxed, almost nonchalant, a soft smile at his lips, his gaze steady. Sort of fellow nobody would have given a second glance, thought Gus, hardly daring to breathe, save for the menace of the Colt he was twirling through his fingers.

Nothing friendly or nonchalant about that.

Joe Fane's sweating had turned him to a mound of grease. Hendy stood motionless, the chewing baccy tight between clenched teeth, his stare cold and hard, tips of his fingers like moths on the table. The clock had ticked on to a minute past noon.

'Now I ain't much for standin' on ceremony,' said Friar, stepping to the bar, the Colt still twirling, 'so we'll make this quick, seein' as how we're expectin' a visitor.'

'Who in hell's name are yuh?' snarled Hendy, his weight easing to the table. 'This is my town, run my way, to *my* law – and you, mister, have been breakin' it at just about every turn! Only ceremony you're ever goin' to stand on—'

Gus Smalley blinked and groaned at the lightning flash of Hendy's hand to his holstered Colt. Joe Fane fell back a step, his arms spreading like wings to hold his balance at the roaring, echoing blaze of the shot from Friar's gun that spun Hendy's piece from his grip to send it clattering across the floor.

'Mite anxious there, Mr Hendy,' drawled Friar, his Colt still levelled and steady. 'Could've taken yuh hand clean off. Yuh head, come to that. Yuh should be a whole lot more careful, yuh know that?'

Hendy mouthed a curse through his grimace as he staunched the flow of blood from his hand.

'Now see here—' began Gus Smalley, gulping on his words as Friar's gun was suddenly aimed at his gut.

'No, mister, you see here. Back up if yuh wanna stay breathin'. You too, braces. And best relieve y'self of that bulge in yuh pocket while yuh at it.' Friar moved carefully round the bar to the batwings and glanced quickly into the street. 'Good – seems like that little diversion's stirred the town some. Whole pack of folk headin' this way.' He grinned. 'Get y'self down here, Mr Brown,' he called. 'We got work to do. Sheriff here can go spend some time in one of them cells of his. Cool him off till I'm in a frame of mind to kill him. Then we can all get to settlin' down to await Marshal Quaid, can't we?' He wiped the back of his hand across his mouth. 'You, fat gut, pour me a drink.'

Joe Fane blinked through a lathering of clinging sweat. Gus Smalley fumbled across the bar for a bottle and glass. Hendy spat the chewing baccy to the floor and sucked his hand nervously.

The clock was ticking to a quarter past the hour

when Brown stepped from the shadowed stairs,
collected Hendy's Colt, Friar's blade, and crossed to
the batwings to watch the approaching line of towns-
folk.

Night train to Utah would be watering up at Forks
Junction about now, he thought. Right on time for
the only passenger waiting there to board it.

'See,' murmured Friar at his side, 'said as how
yuh'd struck it lucky, didn't I?'

It took the folk of Peaceway no more than a short
half-hour, a tirade of fast talking from Morgan Friar
delivered to the accompaniment of the flash of his
twirling Colt from the boardwalk fronting
Mahooney's, and the sight of Sheriff Hendy being
marched to one of his own cells, to realize that if
their town until then had been a frying-pan of fear
and kow-towing to one man's crazed version of the
law, they had been snared in a fire of a hell that
might prove a whole lot worse.

'Anybody wanna leave, he's free to go,' Friar had
drawled as he paced the boards, his piece spinning in
his fingers. 'But he walks as he is. No horses, no trap-
pin's. If you're stayin', yuh here on my terms till I'm
good and ready to pull out.' His grin had been easy,
his gaze tight. 'And I ain't for messin'. As for that
marshal due here, yuh can leave him to m'self and
my partner. He ain't goin' to be your concern.'
Another pause, another twirl, another glare. 'Yuh
should be grateful, all of yuh, I'm riddin' yuh of
Hendy. Yuh standin' in some bad blood there, yuh
know that? Well, I'm sure yuh do, so yuh get to
showin' some respect and gratitude in a manner
fittin'. All right? First man as don't is a dead man

along of the others I had the pleasure of puttin' straight. Now, let's relax, shall we? Have ourselves a quiet day.'

The dazed gathering had stood silent and staring, some open-mouthed, some swallowing, twitching, wondering if this day had ever really dawned. Maybe it was all a dream. Maybe a nightmare.

One man had figured for a wild moment if he might just rush the fellow there, take him off guard – hell, he was only *one* man with a loose-looking gambling type standing to him. What was one man and a gun to a town? He was just that: one man and a gun with no regard for when and where he might use it. Or who might be levelled in his sights. Too handy with that blade along of it.

A bar girl shivering behind the batwings had hardly shifted her gaze from the fellow she had seen beaten and dragged to the jail the night before, the man called simply Brown. Gambling man, she had wondered? Well, maybe. He had the dress – what was left of it – and he had the hands, but that look was something else: sharp, narrowed, the eyes moving like beams that seemed to probe a whole lot deeper than where they settled – when they did.

Fellow with a look like that would be just as sharp with a piece between his fingers as a deck of cards. And the dealing might be a whole lot faster.

And just what, she wondered, was his fascination with the 'breed girl? He was keeping her at his side like she was some long-lost daughter. Taking a shine to a girl was one thing, but owning her . . . still, she had thought, it was that sort of day.

Bart Jessom had left his store unattended and unlocked at the crack of the shots in Mahooney's, his first thought being that Joe Fane had lost his head and figured for himself standing a whole lot taller with Shotts Cutler's Colt in his hand. Sort of crazed thinking Joe would come to pushed too far, but if he had thought for one moment. . . .

No, he was still standing, back of that fellow Friar; and no bulge in his pocket either. Well, not such a loss. Shotts' piece had never fired straight anyhow.

Bart's preoccupation with what Friar had to say had taken him deep into the street, far from his precious counters and the polished glass case where he displayed his gun wares, so that he had no knowledge, minutes later, of the figure passing like a shadow to it, lifting the lid and helping herself.

Lacy Alice had felt markedly better as she scurried back to the old shacks with the gun safe beneath her skirts. Needs must, she had reckoned. And, in any case, Bart Jessom was another with a long-standing unpaid account.

It was an hour into the afternoon when Morgan Friar ordered Beanstalk to down his besom and go make himself useful watching the trail out of Nape Sands for a first sight of Marshal Quaid riding in.

Brown, seated back of the bar, his fingers idling with a pack of cards, had glanced at the clock as Beanstalk hurried away and promptly dealt himself a straight flush.

But patience, he had thought, would be a sight more appropriate game from here on.

TEN

What could a man the likes of Morgan Friar possibly want with a town as two-bit and punch-drunk on its past as Peaceway? Nothing here worth the taking, thought Gus Smalley, wiping the cloth over the same stretch of bar for the twentieth time. And just what, in hell's name was the fellow waiting on? Had to be something or somebody special. He was not pacing there, window to batwings and back again, pausing to scan the street, missing nothing, for the good of his health. Nossir, nothing like.

Morgan Friar had gone to an awful lot of trouble with only one thing in mind: to clear the ground, *his* ground, for a meeting with that visiting Marshal Quaid. He planned on killing him right here in Peaceway, maybe on this very spot, minute the lawman pushed through the wings. And there was nothing and nobody going to stop him.

Gus halted the cloth as the clock struck three. Marshal was late. Should have been here hours back. Or maybe was riding out of the Sands right now; slow and easy, steady pace, figuring he still had all the time he needed before that night train was due.

Maybe they would ship him out decent in a pine box. . . .

'Yuh got an undertaker hereabouts?' drawled Friar, turning through another pacing.

'Sure – sure we have,' mumbled Gus. Charlie Copps sees to the passed on. Always has. Got himself a place—'

'Somebody go tell him I want four coffins and a wagon come sundown,' drawled Friar again, peering over the batwings.

'F-four?' stammered Gus.

'S'right, four. He can count, can't he?'

'Why, sure he can. But I ain't certain—'

'Just do it, fella, before I get to makin' it five,' snapped Friar. He turned from the window to grin at Brown. 'Four should do it, yuh reckon, Mr Brown?'

'I'd reckon,' said Brown without lifting his gaze from the spread of cards in front of him. 'Do just fine.'

Gus swallowed, sweated and wiped his face with the bar cloth. Friar went back to watching the street. Brown played patience.

Joe Fane had slipped clear of the bar and into Mahooney's private back room, closing the door softly behind him as he gulped on a throat as dust-cracked as a dirt floor, blinked the sweat from his eyes and shuddered against the chill of the shadowed gloom.

So he had failed – so what? No disgrace in that, not when you had somebody as professional as Morgan Friar crossing you. And Friar was professional for sure. Could see it in his eyes, way he twirled that Colt like it had grown there in his hand. Professional all

through. Ruthless with it. Think no more of taking
out a fellow than spitting on him.

Hell, how was it that a fellow like that could turn
up here at a time like this, take the town, pen Hendy
and just wait there in the bar cool as a rattler in
shade? What did he want; who did he want? The
town, Hendy, that Marshal Quaid? Was he running
from something, or waiting on it?

Joe blinked again and crossed to Dubs' drinks
cabinet. Locked, of course. Might have known. No
problem. Staying level-headed was the crux for what
he had in mind. Only this time there would be no
guns, no blades. Like he had heard tell some place,
time came when there was only one choice: fight fire
with fire. Sure, just that, till there was nothing of this
town left save the ash of it.

Give it another hour, stay clear of Friar and Brown,
then make it fast to the old shacks. Start the whole
thing there, bring the town scurrying into panic.
Then move on; the store, saloon, jail, rail head. . . .
Anywhere, everywhere. Let Friar fight it out with
Quaid; let Hendy roast, let the whole rotten lot. . . .

Easy there, easy. This needed planning, thinking
through. No rush, no loose moves.

He crossed the room again, this time to the dust-
smeared window overlooking the old shacks – and
stepped quickly to one side, his back to the wall.

Lacy Alice out there and heading this way like she
owned the place!

She rounded the corner at the rooming-house, stood
for a moment in the full glare of the sun, swallowed,
swung her long hair into her neck and tightened her
grip on the butt of the Colt. All or nothing here, she

thought, licking her lips. Face up to Friar, do what she had to do – and pray she was still in one piece come the arrival of that night train.

She stiffened her shoulders and walked on, legs a deal heavier now, it seemed, the sweat on her brow, in her neck beginning to boil. Hell, she had never figured for it ever coming to this. Been in some tight spots in her life, walked as close to the last shadows as the worst of them, talked and manipulated her way into her next breath with all the guile of a cornered rat, but this. . . .

The Colt hung heavy and hot in her hand, a dead weight, fingers wrapped round it like roots. Would she get to lifting it when it mattered most, or would it just hang there, flat as a rock against her thigh? Had she the nerve? She could get to wishing right now she had never set eyes on Friar, made it to the old shacks and stayed there. Wished, too, she had lost her nerve a whole lot earlier right there in Jessom's store, left that lid closed, the gun where it lay.

Too late now. She had the Colt; she had a mind for doing what she knew was right. Sure, but was she going to have the luck?

Alice paused again when she stood before the batwings, her gaze fixed and unblinking on the shadow and smoke-streaked bar beyond them. Times she had flounced through the wings like some tipsy showgirl, all legs and garters, lace frills and smiles; times too when she had staggered out, too manhandled and dazed to know the time of day.

She shivered. Grand entrance, she thought, stepping forward. She might not be a deal fussed about the exit.

'Alice?' croaked Gus Smalley from the far end of

the room. 'What the hell. . . ? What yuh doin' here?
Figured yuh—'

'Friar,' snapped Alice, stiffening against a sudden
twitch in her arm. 'Where is he?' She glanced
quickly, anxiously over the gloom. Back room door
ajar; Gus stood at the bar, clutching a sodden cloth as
if his life depended on it; empty bottle and glasses on
a centre table; Beanstalk's besom propped against
the wall; heeled butts and scattered ash from
discarded cheroots; dust, stained spittoon; shadows,
nothing moving.

'He here?' said Alice, swallowing, the Colt still
leaden in her grip.

'Well, now, if it ain't the town's first lady!'

Alice swung to her right at the clip of the voice
from a corner table, peered for a shape and raised
the Colt.

'Steady there, ma'am,' murmured Brown, laying
aside the cards in his hands. 'I ain't for spoilin' none.
And, 'sides, yuh might miss. Got a young lady here
back of me. Yuh lookin' for her?'

The 'breed girl eased from the shadow, her eyes
wide and wet, lips trembling.

'Just hope yuh ain't abused her none,' snapped
Alice.

'No, ma'am,' said Brown. 'Yuh can lay the blame
for that with yuh one-time sheriff.' He came slowly to
his feet. 'Now, yuh were sayin—'

'I can use this, mister.' Alice gestured with the
Colt. 'And don't think I won't.'

'Never doubted it. Wouldn't be here otherwise,
would yuh?'

'Don't know who yuh really are, mister, and don't
much care. I'm here to—'

'Must be me yuh lookin' for.'

Alice swung again, this time to face the stairway and the darkened, deserted landing at the head of it, her expression tensed and tight, the Colt levelled in a reach that seemed frozen. 'Friar?' she croaked.

'As ever was, ma'am,' came the voice. 'And you are – o'course, comin' back to me now. Can't rightly put a name to yuh, but I recall the place well enough. Beaver Falls? Sure it was.'

Alice blinked at the creak of a floorboard, scuff of a slow step.

'Sometime back, ma'am, but I see time ain't dealt unkindly with yuh. Not one bit.'

'Quaid,' snapped Alice hoarsely. 'Marshal Quaid. Yuh were waitin' on him then same as yuh are now.'

'Ain't you got some memory?' quipped Friar. 'And you're right. Fact is, though, ma'am, me and my partner there got some business a sight more pressin' than Marshal Quaid right now, but seein' as how he's happenin' along of this two-bit town, I dare say I might get to settlin' with him. Be kinda tidy, wouldn't it?'

Alice might then in that moment of the shape appearing above her have raised the Colt a fraction higher and squeezed on the trigger, and she might have got lucky with a single shot, might easily have blown a burning hole clean through Morgan Friar's left leg.

But the Colt stayed leaden and the shape blurred and she felt nothing through her chilled, wooden limbs as the hand settled its grip on her arm and a face closed tight and hot at her cheek.

'This, ma'am, is for your own good,' whispered Brown in her ear. 'Believe me, if yuh wanna stay alive.'

ELEVEN

Steady click of wheels to rails, roll of the car, shift and creak of timber, murmur of a breeze at an open window, flurry of sparks, rush of steam and the grunt of a corner seat, long-distance sleeper tipping his hat at the sunset glare.

'Two hours to Peaceway. Due there at eight and runnin' right to time.'

The ruddy-faced, barrel-bellied conductor eased his way between the seats in the stifled air of the second-class car, nodded to whoever spared him a glance, wiped a glow of sweat from his cheeks and consulted his timepiece with a flourish of chain and flick of the cover.

'Stretch yuh limbs there if yuh've a mind,' he announced. ' 'Bout an hour to fuel and water up.' He closed the timepiece and flourished it back to his waistcoat pocket. 'Two hours to Peaceway,' he called again before leaning closer to the sleeping man in the corner seat. 'Yuh hear that, sir?' he murmured softly.

'I heard,' said the man from beneath the hat.

'Reckoned so,' beamed the conductor. 'Just wanted to be sure.'

The man stretched his legs across the vacant space next to him and tightened his folded arms. 'I'm obliged,' he mumbled.

'No trouble, sir, none at all.' The conductor eased upright again and tapped his timepiece. 'Two hours to Peaceway. . . .'

Fellow there slept tighter than a two-day corpse; never moved, not till now, and then not to show his face. He sick or something? Lud Reemer squirmed his tired shoulders into life, adjusted his coat against the sticky sweat beneath it and narrowed his gaze again on the corner seat sleeper.

So how come a fellow could sleep this long? Hardly shifted a muscle since boarding at Forks Junction. Trail worn perhaps from some tough drive, catching up before he joined his next outfit? Nothing about the cut of his clothes, the smooth, sensitive resting of those long fingers in his lap to suggest some hard-bitten, rough living cattle puncher. Gambling type looking for his next deal? Not here, not riding the rail second-class – not if he was any good. Short haul drifter just chancing his luck on the town, any town, coming up? Well, could be, but a deal too close-shaved and trim for a fellow figuring on his next meal. This fellow lived well enough not to have such concerns.

So maybe he was just sleeping it out to Peaceway. Sure, just that . . . except that any fellow stepping down at Peaceway needed to be watched and accounted for. Well-dressed lone strangers, sleeping or otherwise, were not for losing track of. No telling who they might be or why they might be here. Not this day, and especially not come nightfall.

Reemer nudged the dozing man at his side and leaned closer to his lolling head. 'Yuh payin' any attention here?' he hissed.

The man shuddered, grunted and licked at a dribble of saliva. 'Yuh bet on it,' he croaked, blinking rapidly.

'Sleepin' fella in the corner – what yuh reckon?'

The man blinked again and stiffened his shoulders. 'Don't reckon him for nothin',' he murmured, lifting a bushy eyebrow.

'Well, mebbe yuh should. He's leavin' the train at Peaceway.'

'So mebbe he lives there.'

'Fella the look of him don't *live* nowhere. They happen. I seen 'em before. They got a way with 'em.'

The man grunted and wiped a hand over his stubble.

'They all got a way with 'em in your eyes, Reemer,' he grinned. 'All hell-raisin' lawmen, ain't they? All stalkin' yuh like some pack of big cats. Know your trouble, fella? I'll tell yuh what's eatin' at yuh. . . .'

But Lud Reemer was not listening. He was back to watching the sleeping fellow and the eye he was certain had opened in the shadow of the tipped hat.

Charlie Hicks's fingers drummed lightly across the lid of his pocketed timepiece as he squinted against the glare of the setting sun from the swaying observation platform of the first-class car. He was hot, sweating fit to melt, and for the only time in five years as conductor on the Gratton to Morriston overnight express regretting ever coming to within so much as a whiff of a railroad.

And not surprising, he reckoned, brushing at a

swirl of smuts from a twist of smoke. Goddamn it, old Engine 37 up there was hauling a keg of dynamite!

Figure it: a freight car packed tight with crates marked Bank of Western Central, and no guessing what lay beneath the lids neither, not after a glance at the half-dozen fellows travelling along of them. Not the first time, of course. Western Central had shipped west to Utah on the overnight any number of times, but this, a whole car for crates and guards was big, a sight bigger than Charlie Hicks had ever seen in all his railroad years.

And that had been more than enough to set him sweating before 37 had raised a head of steam.

But that had been only the half of it. He had five fellows riding second-class who looked about as friendly as a nest of rattlers waiting on their supper. Word out of place among the likes of them – a side-long glance would suffice – and somebody might be wishing he had reckoned a deal closer on riding the long-haul stage. Only consolation being, he figured, the five would be stepping down at Peaceway.

First-class seemed as quiet as the night: flush cattle-man, two gamblers, a prim army officer's wife and her daughter destined for Fort Benton, hotel propri-etor speculating on a venture at Morriston, and the pale-faced fellow in the dark suit with the fancy trim who looked as if he should have stayed where he belonged, somewhere back East.

And then there was the passenger who had climbed aboard at Forks Junction.

Sure, thought Charlie, running a finger beneath the grip of his sweat-soaked collar, there was him, the soft-spoken, slow-eyed lawman who had taken him aside soon as he had boarded, introduced himself as

Marshal Quaid and said as how he was not for being known. 'Just keep me briefed on where we are and let me sleep. Nothin' else. Yuh understand?'

Seemed reasonable, Charlie had thought. Marshal wanted to stay low, he could do just that.

'Fine,' Quaid had smiled, then added carefully, 'Oh, and yuh don't pull out of Peaceway 'ceptin' on my say-so. That clear?'

No, that was not one bit clear, damn it! Railroad owners back at Gratton might have something to say about that – *would* have a whole lot to say about that – not to mention the passengers and Taffs, the engineer, who never ceased to remind that Engine 37 was no filly. 'She's past her best and needs some coaxin' to a start up.'

The marshal had said nothing; simply stared, grunted, settled himself in the corner seat and tipped his hat against the glare.

And there was another thing, pondered Charlie, flicking at another rush of smuts, how come a full-fledged marshal travelled second-class, and how come he had boarded the train at a rundown whistle-stop the likes of Forks Junction? Where had he come from?

More to the point, what nature of business was it the marshal had to tend in Peaceway that could possibly delay the night train, especially a night train packed tight with the assets of Western Central?

Hell – the crates back there, five fellows brooding fit to twitch out of their skins, a sleeping marshal. . . . One hour, fifty minutes to Peaceway.

Seemed to Charlie Hicks, sweating in the sunset glare, like a lifetime.

*

Lud Reemer's thoughts were drifting to the prospect of a life of easy comforts some place deep in Mexico where folk would greet him with respect, good-looking women sit at his feet and he had the time, all the time in the world, to count his fortune daily, piece by shining piece.

Some satisfaction to be had in that, he reckoned; a prospect with shapes he could fathom and shadows he could understand. . . . Unlike the shape and shadow slumped in that corner seat.

Fellow had still not shifted, still had his hat tipped low, and was still, he would have sworn, keeping one eye open. Well, never mind the eye, or what it was watching. Just keep his own on the fellow when this grinding heap of iron pulled into Peaceway. It would be then and there that he needed watching.

You could never tell with a fellow like that, not when the night was settling and he might slip away like a shadow.

Or be the one that stayed.

TWELVE

The trembling glimmer of light from a freshly primed lantern lifted the shadows in Mahooney's bar until only the corners lay in darkness. The clock's dull tick seemed as measured as footfalls. Somebody coughed, a boot scraped, a chair creaked.

Gus Smalley shifted a half-empty bottle a fraction to the right, then back again to the same circle of stain, his fingers shaking as they slid away. Lacy Alice crossed her legs, folded her arms and stared defiantly at the man at the batwings. The 'breed girl shivered at her side and pulled nervously at the rags of her dress. The card player in the darkest corner cracked open a new pack, removed the joker and placed it face up to his left.

Then nobody moved or dared to breathe as they waited on the man hurrying down the street, mounting the boardwalk, pausing a moment before scurrying to the wings and the shaft of yellow light.

'Well?' croaked Friar, his gaze tight on Beanstalk's sweat-lathered face. 'Yuh see him?'

'Not a hint of no rider out there, Mr Friar, sir,' spluttered the man. 'Ain't a hint of nothin', far as yuh can see. And yuh can't see a deal at all right now, not this time of day yuh can't. Be hard pushed—'

'All right, all right,' snapped Friar, slapping a hand across the wings. 'Yuh just keep lookin', yuh hear?'

'But Mr Friar, sir, there ain't nothin'—'

'Do it, damn yuh! Just do it.'

'Yuh got it wrong,' smiled Alice from the far end of the bar. 'He ain't goin' to show. There ain't goin' to be no Marshal Quaid in Peaceway, not this day there ain't. Now I wonder why?'

'Don't need no opinion from you,' scowled Friar, turning from the wings.

'Bet yuh don't at that,' smiled Alice again. 'But what about yuh partner here? He know about Quaid? Yuh told him? Doubt that somehow.' She uncrossed her legs, stretched her arms to her hips and came to her feet. 'What yuh reckon, Mr Brown? Yuh figure for that marshal ridin' in?'

'Don't take no note of her,' snapped Friar. 'She's talkin' out of her neck. Quaid ain't of no concern. If he shows, he shows. I'll handle it. No problem.'

'Could be he's here, o'course,' mocked Alice, crossing to lean on the bar. 'Yuh thought of that? Mebbe he's somewhere right now, watchin' yuh.'

'Yuh wanna stay on them pretty legs of yours, yuh'd best keep yuh mouth shut,' growled Friar.

'Suit y'self,' sighed Alice, reaching for the half-empty bottle and a glass. 'Me – well, I'd be wonderin'.'

Gus Smalley swallowed, sweated and glanced at the clock. 'An hour to the night train,' he murmured, blinking and squinting.

Brown pushed the cards aside and stretched as he eased from the table. 'Time flies, don't it?' he grinned. 'Waits on no man, does it?'

Friar grunted. Alice poured herself a drink.

Beanstalk wandered back to the darkening street and was already heading for his look-out in the smoky remains of the livery when Bart Jessom slid from his store to the shadows, a Winchester tight in his grip, and padded like a skulking dog towards the jail.

He had a plan, sound as a rock, and he had a gun. All he needed.

Joe Fane brushed a shred of cobwebs from the brim of his hat, a flaking of dust from his stubble, hitched his braces over the cold sweat across his shoulders and eased the door of the old shack open a fraction wider.

Clear view from here to the top of the street, Sheriff Hendy's office, the rail head, corral and scattering of crates, wagons, timbers and thrown aside trash cluttering this end of town.

Perfect, he thought, just perfect. Flame started there, with the soft night breeze blowing north to south, and Peaceway would be. . . . Hell, only one word for it: ash.

He smiled, licked his cracked lips and narrowed his gaze on the shadowed, silent sprawl of the station, Sam Wards' office, the gleaming reach of the track to the thickening night.

Awful quiet up there, he mused; no sounds, no movements, and no light in Sam's office. How come? Train was due in an hour. Not like Sam to be waiting on it in the dark. Fellow treated the head and track through it like he owned the spread. Took a personal pride in the place. Sam Ward *was* the railroad hereabouts, so how was it. . . ?

Joe swallowed slowly. How was it, damn it, Sam had not been seen all day? How come he had not been helping at the livery fire, not there in the bar to see Hendy shoot Mac Ives in cold blood, not there when that fellow Friar had shown himself? And, come to think of it, how was it. . . ?

Joe swallowed again, eased the door wider and slid from the broken cobwebs like a careful fly.

It took only minutes for him to reach the corral, slide along its darker side and sidle into the mound of crates and timbers flanking the steps to the platform. He was a while longer contemplating the move to Sam's office. No cover once onto the steps, and supposing there was somebody already there in the office?

Forget it. Just do it.

He slid softly, silently along the platform, eyes flicking anxiously, hands and cheeks wet with sweat. 'Sam – yuh there?' he hissed, regretting the sound the second he had made it. He waited, listened, moved again; slow, shuffling steps now until he had reached the door to the office.

His hand was shaking as he reached for the knob, settled on it, waited, then softly as if fearful it might bite, turned it and pushed the door open.

It creaked back on the silent, shadow-deep office where the shapes of Sam's counter, his telegraph corner, chair, cabinet, chest of drawers, stood black as a flock of crows, where nothing moved and the only sound was the murmured tick of the clock.

'Sam,' hissed Joe again. 'Yuh there? What the hell's—'

The tip of his boot pushed against the sprawled body before he saw it, and was already sticky with congealing blood when Joe summoned the guts to bend lower and peer into the death-grey, bulging-eyed face of Sam Wards.

Somebody had cut his throat long back, left him in the pools of his own blood, closed the door carefully and disappeared. Had all the marks of Morgan Friar, thought Joe, gulping on a mounting bile. Done the same for Sam as he had for Mahooney.

He had stepped back, sweat-soaked and shivering, to the deserted platform, his mind reeling, thoughts stabbing like ice, when the roar of the rifle shot at Hendy's office shattered the night silence.

'Now you just listen up real close there, Hendy,' croaked Bart Jessom, sweat dripping from his chin, his gaze wide and wild, 'I ain't blasted the lock on that cell door there for the hell of it.' His grip on the rifle tightened as he prodded the barrel at the sheriff's gut. 'Nothin' like. Yuh understand? You and me got some figurin' to do here, and fast.'

'I'm hearin' yuh, Bart,' said Hendy, sliding clear of the cell and the drifting smear of gunsmoke to the gloom of his office. ' 'Ceptin' I wasn't reckonin' on nobody doin' what yuh just done there.' He glanced quickly at the twisted, cordite-smeared remains of the cell lock. 'Amazin' ain't it, what close-aimed lead can do? Amazin'. . . . Yuh were sayin'?'

'I'm sayin' as how time's runnin' out for this town and most of us in it.' Jessom swallowed. 'That fella Friar back there. . . .' He swallowed again and narrowed his gaze to dark slits. 'Yuh reckon yuh could take him? Yuh figure?'

Hendy shrugged. 'If I had a piece—' he began.

'I gotta piece back at the store,' snapped Jessom.

'It's yours – *if* yuh go use it on Friar and that creepin' gamblin' type along of him. What yuh say?' He licked his lips. 'Can't say as how I'm for yuh runnin' this town as yuh been doin', but I'm a realist, mister, a businessman. Better the devil I know, than the sonofabitch back there who might do anythin'. Well?'

'Sure,' grinned Hendy, 'show me the piece. I still got one good hand, Be a pleasure, Mr Jessom.' The grin slanted. 'Like yuh say, time's runnin' out.'

THIRTEEN

A window rattled; a door slammed; somebody shouted a throaty curse; lights glowed to life behind pinched black panes, and Gus Smalley's back creaked as he stiffened and glanced anxiously first at the bar girls hovering in a clutch of arms and shaking hands at the top of the stairs, then at Friar, Brown and a smugly relaxed Lacy Alice.

'Hear that? Winchester shot. Sheriff's office. Somebody's sprung Hendy,' drawled Alice almost tiredly. 'Yuh should've figured on that, Morgan. Likes of that scum don't stay penned for long. Now what yuh goin' to do? Me, I'd—'

'One more word outa you, lady, and I'll slit yuh throat wide as the street!' snapped Friar, crossing to the wings. 'Go take a look, Mr Brown. Finish it. We ain't got the time for messin' with crazed sheriffs.'

Brown grunted, tossed his rifle from hand to hand and came quietly to Friar's side. 'T'ain't for me to say, o'course,' he murmured at the man's ear, 'but lookin' at the way things are in strictly gamblin' terms, I'd reckon for the odds here beginnin' to stack wrong side of the baize.'

Friar's eyes gleamed. 'What's that supposed to mean?'

'Hendy on the loose again – so somebody figures him for bein' a safer bet than you – no sign of that marshal, train due in under the hour. . . . Don't it occur yuh might not have this town as tight as yuh figured?'

'Tight enough,' said Friar, his gaze drifting watchfully to the still deserted street. 'My boys out at Nape Sands'll be here with the wagons time it takes you to settle with Hendy. Rail head's all quiet – I taken care of that – and as for the snivellin' folk here, I ain't countin' on them bein' no bother.'

' 'Cept for whoever's just got to Hendy.' Brown slid a hand slowly down the barrel of the rifle. 'And, o'course, that marshal. Been a sight more decent of yuh to have mentioned yuh personal feud with him. How come yuh didn't? He spook yuh some?'

'Quaid?' scoffed Friar. 'He ain't worth a spit. Sure, I know him. Known him from way back. Crossed him more than once – and if there's so much as a hair of a chance of killin' him, that's fine by me. Just fine. I'll handle it.' His gaze came back to Brown. 'Real gilt on the pot hearin' he was due here,' he grinned. 'Never bargained for that, but when yuh look at it. . . . Well, Mr Brown, who wouldn't grab at a chance of buryin' some bad bones of the past at the same time as he's helpin' himself to his new future? Who wouldn't, eh? Like I say, real gilt. Now, yuh goin' to get to Hendy? Clock's still tickin'.'

It was a full minute then before Friar turned from watching Brown's disappearance into the night to face Lacy Alice. 'Neat as a button,' he smiled. 'All goin' exactly to plan.'

'All except Quaid,' said Alice, helping herself to another drink. 'I'll bet he ain't goin' one bit as planned. But, then, he never did, did he?'

Gus Smalley's back creaked again as the shadows seemed to blur Friar's grin to a twitching slant.

Brown had melted to the shadows in the few fast steps it had taken for him to slip from the boardwalk to the alley at the side of the saloon.

He waited, his back tight to the wall, the Winchester easy in his grip, eyes moving through a slow, piercing gaze. Lights still glowing in a dozen or more windows, he noted; anxious faces peering and probing behind them, searching for the source of the shot that had echoed through the night like the spit of some old ghost. Who had dared to fire a shot, and why? Who still had the nerve to be carrying a gun? Somebody was out there. Somebody was moving, somewhere.

Only a matter of time now, thought Brown, before one of the faces at one of the windows summoned the guts to go take a look, head for the jail end of town . . . be right there as Hendy swaggered back to *his* street in *his* town.

Brown flexed his fingers in his grip on the rifle, crossed the alley to the next patch of shadow and waited again, his gaze focused now on the black brooding windows at Jessom's store. Been a light there, sure enough, he thought. Nothing so certain as a lantern glow; no more than a sudden flare, a hovering flicker, then nothing. But the shadows had moved. Too right they had. The merest drift of something passing behind glass; a shape there in one moment, gone in the next.

Jessom collecting his day's take from the cash drawer, checking out the stock? Not after a day such as Peaceway had witnessed! Only stock worth checking out. . . . Guns, damn it! Jessom held a full hand in town where weapons of any shape or size were concerned.

Brown had moved again, two steps to the deepest shadows sprawling across the street, when the click of a latch, murmur of hushed voices, soft closing of a door at the rear of the store, forced him to scurry like a whipped dog back to the alley.

His grip on the Winchester had tightened in two hands as he watched Hendy skulk through the night to the boardwalk opposite Mahooney's bar, a Colt planted deep in his belt.

'Friar – know yuh in there. I'm waitin' on yuh. Time for me to get back to runnin' my town. Yuh hear me, Friar? I'm waitin'.'

Hendy's voice snapped like the crack of new leather as he lounged his weight to one hip, hooked the thumb of his bandaged hand in his belt and drummed the fingers of the other lightly on his thigh.

Taking some chance there, thought Brown. Straight shooting showdown with a gunslinger as fast as Friar was hardly Hendy's style. More for stacking the deck to himself and dealing from the bottom.

'Friar – yuh gettin' cold feet back there? Want for me to come and get yuh?'

Nothing moving in the bar, no creep of shadow to the boardwalk, no dimming of the light. Friar going to sit it out, wondered Brown, just wait there? More to the point, did he have the time? Night train was due in thirty minutes.

'Friar – yuh hearin' me?'

He was hearing you sure enough, mused Brown, loud and clear – and leaving the silence to answer.

The drumming fingers had lost their rhythm, the weight shifted, hooked thumb slid from the belt as the hand loosened, then tightened, closing to a clench. Impatience, uncertainty, growing fear? The line of sweat beading Hendy's upper lip said as much as the narrowed glare of the gaze.

Creak of the batwings, scuff of a soft step.

Hendy tensed, shoulders stiffening, fingers flexing anxiously. But still no drift of shadow to the board-walk, nothing to hint at where Friar was or where he might be coming from.

Brown swallowed. Chances were Friar was waiting on his 'gambling' partner making a move; wondering if he was out there right now, Winchester levelled and steady, all set to blaze on Hendy's first reach for that belted Colt.

Another creak, another step.

This was going to be resolved in a whirlwind, a swirl of hands, rage and roar of lead. No words, no quarter; only the piercing gleam of eyes in the moment when hot fingers pressed tight on cold steel.

Or was it? Hendy was moving now, slipping step by slow step to his right, into deeper shadow, away from the direct line of the bar-room glow. What the hell. . . . Somebody behind him. Bart Jessom, damn it, hovering in a shaking mound of sweat, set to step into Hendy's place, leaving the sheriff free to cross the street, mount the boardwalk fronting the bar and

glide like a rattler along the wall as Friar broke
through the wings.

Dealing from the bottom of the pack. . . . 'See
about that,' murmured Brown, easing from the alley
to the street.

He waited, catching the muffled crunch of
Hendy's dash to the boardwalk, glancing quickly at
Jessom as he began to shuffle into place, freezing at
the sound of a door opening and closing with a thud,
hushed urgent voices, and then, as if slicing the darkness, the louder, faster creak of the wings being flung
open.

Brown was into the street in one slithering rush,
twisting to swing the rifle round to the looming
shape of Hendy, his Colt drawn on Friar as he strad-
dled the boards and peered for a sight of his target
but saw only the sweat-soaked, quaking shape of the
storekeeper.

'Get back! Get the hell out!' growled Brown, the
Winchester roaring into life to lift a spray of splinters
from the timbers at Hendy's feet.

Friar crashed back to the wings. Hendy cursed, his
blaze scudding to the sidewalk roof, eyes flashing as
they settled on Brown, the glinting probe of the
barrel, fingers working frantically on the Colt.

The Winchester roared again, deep and loud now
so that the echo groaned across the night. Hendy
stumbled at the first blaze, staggered, slid to the wall,
bounced clear and was still stumbling on when
Brown blazed again, this time with his teeth clenched
as if willing the lead into fury.

Hendy collapsed to his knees, the Colt loose in his
fingers, mouth opening, lips twisting, but was a full
half-minute before he hit the boards, twitched once

and lay still, his stare wide on the smoke-hazed street and the man commanding it.

'Said as how yuh were my man,' drawled Friar, pushing open the wings. 'But that, my friend, was close,' he added, an eyebrow lifting on a red-rimmed gaze.

'So's that night train,' said Brown, relaxing the rifle. 'And in case yuh ain't noticed, we seem to be the only ones waitin' on it. Bar back of yuh is empty.'

He stepped to the boardwalk, kicked Hendy's Colt clear of the dead man's fingers, and sighed. 'Ain't nobody goin' to miss that scum – assumin' there's anybody still about to notice.'

His gaze swung back to the deserted street. 'Who's dealin' now, Mr Friar?'

FOURTEEN

'Twenty minutes to Peaceway. Twenty minutes. . . .'

Charlie Hicks swallowed on a dusty, bone-dry throat, flourished his timepiece importantly, pocketed it and leaned closer to the sleeping man in the corner seat.

'Yuh care to step outa the car for a moment, sir, there's somethin' I figure yuh should see,' he whispered, one eye glancing back to the other passengers.

The man raised his hat a fraction from his face, grunted softly and let the brim fall again to the bridge of his nose.

'Yuh hear that, folks?' smiled Charlie, opening the door to the carriage platform. 'Peaceway comin' up.'

Lud Reemer prodded an elbow into the ribs of the man seated next to him. 'Gettin' close. Yuh all set?'

'I been set for days,' said the man, squirming his aching shoulders. 'Yuh ain't still frettin' on that fella there, are yuh?'

'He ain't shifted hardly a muscle. Nobody sleeps that good.'

'So mebbe he's tired,' sighed the man.

'Watchin' more like. That tipped hat don't fool me none. I seen fellas—'

87

'Sure yuh have. We heard it all before, Lud, many times!' The man rolled his shoulders again. 'He troubles yuh that much,' he murmured, 'I'll make certain he gets a bullet early. How's that?'

'Assumin' he don't get to yuh first. Yuh seen that Colt he's packin'? Piece like that ain't no decoration. He knows how to use it.'

'Yeah, yeah,' soothed the man, 'yuh bet he does. Well, mebbe we should tell the rest of the boys, eh?'

'I'm tellin' yuh,' clipped Lud. 'Nobody sleeps that good.'

The man eased his butt and straightened his hat. 'Glad we got yuh along of us, Lud. Savin' us a whole heap of effort with all that worryin' yuh doin'. Fair exhausts me, darned if it don't!'

Reemer scowled and ran his hands over his knees, but his eyes were narrowed tight and probing as the man in the corner seat stirred, came to his feet and passed without a word or glance to the carriage platform.

'Somethin' ain't right out there,' said Charlie, bracing himself against the rush of night air, the swirl of smoke and flying sparks. 'Take a look for y'self, Marshal. What yuh see? Or mebbe I should ask, what *don't* yuh see?'

Quaid leaned from the platform and squinted into the sweep of land hugged tight in the cloak of darkness, the sprawl of cloud thickening on the drift of the moon, the lift of a distant hill range and the darker, brooding bulks of the town of Peaceway. 'Town comin' up fast,' he called against the rattle of the train, the rhythmic click of wheels on rails, heaving chug of the locomotive.

'Sure,' said Charlie, moving closer to the marshal's ear, 'that's Peaceway – know the approach like the back of my hand – but I ain't never seen it in near total darkness, and I ain't never seen that rail head there without so much as a glimmer of light.' He flicked a hand at a twist of smuts. 'Sam Wards ain't one for hidin' his station. Usually got the place decked out fit to blind yuh. So what's wrong t'night? And why's the town black as an undertaker's coat? That ain't right neither. Don't make no sense, not with the train due in ten minutes it don't.'

Quaid continued to squint, the skin at his cheeks stretched tight to the bone. 'What yuh figure?' he asked, wincing at a swish of chilled air.

'Figure a whole heap of things, but t'ain't for me to speculate none, is it? All I'm sayin' is, somethin's wrong. That rail head just ain't as it should be. Had my way, I'd pass straight through, no stoppin', but that ain't in the regulations and we need to water up.'

Quaid leaned back and fastened his gaze on Charlie's face. 'Yuh right, it ain't in no regulations,' he drawled. 'Yuh pull in as normal, nothin' different.'

'Yuh got any idea of what we're haulin' back there, Marshal? I'll tell yuh—'

'I know exactly what you're haulin',' said Quaid, 'but it ain't just a fortune in gold yuh got to fret over.'

'Yuh know about the gold? That why yuh here?'

'Train stops like it always does,' snapped the marshal.

The sigh behind Charlie Hicks's shrug was lost in the piercing blast and echoing shriek of Engine 37's warning whistle.

*

Lacy Alice waited, her gaze lifted to the high night sky above the charred rafters of the burned-out livery, listened for a moment to the echo of the night train's whistle, then moved on, ushering the half-breed and the bar girls into the depths of the still smoke-streaked shadows.

Gus Smalley stumbled through the debris to her side and wiped the cold sweat from his face. 'That's thirty-seven rattlin' in on time,' he croaked. 'Yuh figure for Friar bein' at the rail head?'

'Seems like that's what he's here for, don't it?' said Alice. 'God knows why, but he ain't here as no passenger, that's for sure.' She stifled a creeping shiver and hugged herself. 'Awful anxious to get Hendy outa the way, weren't he? Hell. . . .' She shivered again and tightened the hug. 'Went down like the dirt-scrubbin' hog he was. Bled like it too. Sonofabitch!'

'But just who's that fella Brown?' frowned Gus. 'Gamblin' types don't handle a piece like he does. Yuh reckon he's—'

'I don't reckon nothin', Gus, save that Morgan Friar's got this town by the scruff of its neck, and believe me, that's about as bad as havin' Hendy's filthy hands on it. I know, I crossed Friar before. He ain't no saviour.' Alice turned her gaze to the night beyond the ruins. 'Only chance now is for that Marshal Quaid to get himself here, and fast.'

'And just where the hell is he?' groaned Gus. 'Mebbe he ain't comin'. Mebbe he weren't never comin'.'

'Oh, he's comin',' said Alice softly. 'You bet on it.

I know he is. I got that feelin'.' She turned again, her eyes brightening, lips set to a determined line. 'Meantime, there's now and the girls here. We gotta keep them—'

Gus swung round and staggered back through the debris at the sound of spinning wheels, creaking timbers and pounding hoofs.

'What the hell in tarnation is that?' he mouthed, as he watched the rushing blur of hitched, lathered teams, swaying wagons, drivers heaving on the reins, grow on the darkness and moonlit trail out of Nape Sands like racing phantoms.

'Them's Clancy Springs' outfits,' he croaked, his eyes wet and bulging. 'Headin' for the rail head.'

'Joinin' up with Friar,' said Alice, clambering to Gus's side. Her bright gaze narrowed. 'Why? For what?' She laid a hand on the man's arm. 'We gotta get ourselves armed. We need guns.'

'Damnit, Alice, we ain't no gunfighters, none of us. And where we goin' to get guns, and even if we do—'

'Jessom's store. Some still there. I seen 'em.'

'Yeah, yeah, so I get to the store, lift the guns, then what? Yuh ain't thinkin' of standin' to Friar?'

'Don't know what's goin' on round here,' hissed Alice. 'Don't know why or whose guns levelled where, but I sure as hell got a gut feeling we're goin' to find ourselves slap in the middle of it – with nowhere to go!'

Gus blinked, swallowed and stared like a jack-rabbit rooted to the spot at the shimmering blaze of Engine 37's headlight as it probed the silent, shadowed bulk of the deserted rail head.

FIFTEEN

It was the night train Friar was here for, thought Bart Jessom, staring blankly into the shadows; nothing else, not the town, the folk, not even Hendy. Just the train and being here to meet it in his way, on his terms, for whatever sonofabitch reason had festered back of the gunslinger's mind.

And it was going to take no more than a few short minutes for that clanking heap of steam-stained steel and grease-smooth iron to roll in, hiss to a halt and for Friar and his gambling partner to step aboard and get to whatever it was they rated worth so much effort.

Five short, ground-rumbling minutes, and then old Engine 37 would brake up tight as a tick in warm blankets.

Bart twitched in the ache of his limbs, the thudding in his head, the sting behind his watering, bloodshot eyes, and pressed himself tight to the shadows of the old shacks at the rail head.

His thoughts were still reeling from the gunning of Hendy, the way that fellow Brown had slid from the dark like some fiery-eyed cat and blazed his Winchester, steady, levelled, deadly. And not for the

92

first time, reckoned Bart. Nossir, Brown might shuffle a deck with a velvet touch, but his hands were dirt raw when it came to a shooting.

And, hell, two swigs from a bottle to a barrel, it could have been himself plumb in the firing line! Fool plan from the start. Should never have figured on it, could have got himself killed – but Hendy had gone down, damn it, and Peaceway would be a whole lot cleaner for that.

'Yeah, a whole lot,' he mumbled to himself, easing from the shadow for a closer look at the searing blaze of the headlight as the night train began to slow its approach.

Blast of the whistle, grinding screech of wheels at the rails, the thunderous rumble of the locomotive, spitting steam, flying sparks, final thrust of clouding smoke. . . . Four minutes.

Bart pressed his shoulders to the wall of the shack, licked his lips, blinked and eased again for a closer look at the main street heading back to town. Place was quiet enough now. Folk too scared to move, he guessed, fearful that Friar's fingers might get to twitching again; gun or blade, end result was the same.

Still a glow of light at Mahooney's; twist of slow, thin smoke from the livery; his own place in darkness; sheriff's office dead as its one-time occupant. Quietest he had seen Peaceway in years. But scratch the surface. . . .

Where the hell had Joe Fane buried himself, he wondered in a sudden surge of cold sweat at his neck, and where was Gus, Lacy Alice, the 'breed girl, bar girls, not to mention Marshal Quaid? And another thing, he thought, swinging his gaze back to the rail head, how come the station was still in darkness, and where was Sam?

And now what, in the name of all Creation, was this: two wagons swinging to the rail head from out of Nape Sands, swirling the dust like they were in some race against time? Clancy's outfits, sure enough, but definitely not Clancy's men at the reins.

They something to do with whatever Friar and Brown had planned, frowned Bart? Here because of that night train trundling in, only two minutes away?

'Step back real slow, and don't take one breath more than necessary.'

Bart swallowed, pushed himself from the wall and turned slowly. 'Joe?' he croaked. 'What the hell yuh doin' here? What in tarnation—'

'Don't ask,' hissed Joe Fane, moving a step closer. 'Not yet. Not till I'm good and ready. There ain't the time. We got other matters to tend.'

'We? What yuh mean, *we*? I ain't—'

'Yes yuh are, Bart. Comin' with me all the way on this. I got it figured.' The grin at Joe's lips slanted to a wet twitch. His eyes gleamed. 'Train there's about to make its very last stop at Peaceway. It's a fact, Bart. And yuh know why? I'll tell you – 'cus next time it's steamin' down the line there ain't goin' to be no Peaceway! Just the ash of it.'

'No regrets, Mr Brown?' quipped Morgan Friar, flicking his steely, shafted gaze through the shadows to the man at his side. 'I should say not! Best hand yuh held in a long whiles, ain't it?' His grin spread to a soft, easy smile. 'Minutes away from a fortune, just as long as it takes for that old iron horse out there to roll right up to yuh feet. So how's it feel? What's goin' through yuh mind? Bet you're makin' some real fancy plans, eh?'

Brown nodded and shifted his feet again.

'There's six fellas guardin' the gold last but one freight car. They'll be stretchin' their legs, takin' the air, soon as the train pulls in. Minute that car door slides open, my boys – five of 'em travellin' second class – make their move.' Friar's stare darkened. 'We ain't takin' prisoners. Right? Nobody – no guards, no passengers, first-class included. Any questions?'

'What if the train don't stop?' asked Brown. 'Yuh got this place in darkness. T'ain't natural.'

'Night train waters up at Peaceway. It'll stop.'

'And later – what then?' said Brown.

'Gold's loaded on the wagons drawn up back of yuh and we head out to the Sands. Clancy Springs' place, 'ceptin' there ain't no Clancy no more. He's long dead.' Friar's grin spread like a stain. 'Yuh'll get your share there. Somethin' extra along of it for takin' out Hendy. I owe yuh on that.'

Brown cradled the Winchester and turned his gaze to the dark, deserted spread of the town. 'Let's hope they stay quiet,' he murmured.

'Root spooked, ain't they?' smiled Friar. 'We done a good job. Anybody fool enough to get to nosyin' now. . . . Yuh could handle it, couldn't yuh?'

'Sure,' said Brown, his eyes narrowing against the thickening glare of the headlight. 'Tell yuh somethin' else. . . .'

But his words were drowned in the blast of Engine 37's final call, the clang of its bell and shrieking grind of skidding wheels.

Charlie Hicks's fingers fumbled on a shaking hand as

he tried for the third time to pocket his timepiece
and grab the rail for his swing from the car platform
to the boardwalk station.

Heck, he thought, twisting his neck against his
sweat-soaked collar, he had been doing this for years,
more times than he cared to remember: just standing
here, checking the time, waiting on that last slither of
wheels as 37 ground to a halt, catching the hiss of
steam, chatter of passengers anxious to step down,
sight of Sam Ward scuttling from his office. . . .

Hell, no Sam, not the flicker of a light; nothing
save the darkness, the sprawl of deep shadows, and
just no telling, not a hint of what might be lurking in
any one of them.

Nothing for it, best warn them fellows back there
with the gold not to move, sit tight, wait till Marshal
Quaid said as how it was clear. . . .

Damn it, that sonofabitch lawman had disappeared, slipped away before the train had stopped.
Now what?

Tell you now what, groaned Charlie to himself,
there were two fellows stepping out of the shadows
who looked about as likely night train passengers to
Utah as hound dogs from a back alley.

Charlie's fingers were still fumbling when he saw
the levelled guns.

SIXTEEN

'Don't do it, Joe. Don't even think it, not yet, not 'til we figured this through.' Bart Jessom's lathered face glistened like a ball of glass in the stifling darkness of the dusty shack, his eyes swimming and blinking, lips trembling round the words that grated in his throat. 'We can't be certain. . . . Hell, we just don't know what's happenin', not for sure we don't.'

'I can see what's happenin',' scowled Joe. 'I got eyes, same as you. I seen what that sonofabitch did to Sam. I stood in the blood of it, damn it. And I can sure as hell see now, can't I? It's the train, Bart. Morgan Friar's takin' the train!'

'Mebbe, mebbe,' spluttered Bart, 'but torchin' the town ain't goin' to stop him now. Too late for that, Joe. Only cuttin' yuh nose there to spite yuh face.' He slapped a wet, sticky hand round his neck and flicked the sweat aside. 'There's gotta be another way. Gotta be.'

Joe Fane slid to the half-open door and squinted into the night. 'Train's pulled in. Friar's there, that fella Brown along of him. Whole bunch of scumbags steppin' down.' He hissed and spat. 'Retribution, ain't no other word for it. Sidin' with Hendy like we did, goin' along with him and his way for the sake of

our own skins, them killin's and hangin's. . . .
Retribution. Town don't deserve to stand. Should be
wiped from the face of the earth – and mebbe us with
it!'

'The wagons!' snapped Bart, stumbling to Joe's
side. 'Clancy Springs' outfits drawn up there. They
gotta figure in this somewhere, so mebbe we should
get to them.'

'Yuh mean torch 'em?' said Joe. 'Drivers ain't with
them now. They've moved off to join Friar. Mebbe we
could get close, slip the teams—'

'Then torch 'em, just like yuh say. Yuh reckon?'

Joe spat again. 'What we waitin' for?'

'Don't nobody move. Not a muscle.'

Brown's gaze moved with the slow, careful range of
the Winchester over the staring, wide-eyed passengers in the first-class car. He gestured with a shift of
the barrel for Charlie Hicks to join them. 'Now yuh
listen up, all of yuh,' he said quickly. 'There ain't
goin' to be the time for sayin' it twice.'

'Just what the hell is this?' coughed the florid
faced cattleman, flattening his hands across his
paunch.

'A hold-up. Simple as that,' said a gambling man,
scattering a pack of cards to the table at his side.

'If it's money yuh want—' began the hotel proprietor.

'What else, f'Cris'sake?' snapped the gambling
man's partner. 'He ain't here for his health.'

'I got money,' spluttered the pale-faced fellow. 'I
got it. Right here.' He made to reach for a brocade
valise.

'Leave it,' clipped Brown.

'This is an outrage, an outrage, I say,' piped the elderly woman, twisting her fingers through a shawl at her shoulders. 'I'll have you know, young man, that my husband is Colonel Royston Langster of the Seventh, and when he gets to hear of this. . . . Stop snivellin', Letitia,' she snapped, flashing a hawk-sharp look at the tall, skinny girl cringing behind her.

'Tell yuh somethin' else,' drawled the paunchy cattleman, 'my boys back out the Bar Nine ain't goin' to be one bit happy anythin' happens to me. Tell yuh that for nothin', mister. My boys ain't for messin'.'

'Hold it, folks,' said Charlie Hicks. 'Hold it right there. Mebbe we should do as the fella says – stay put and hear him out.'

'Sure,' mouthed the gambling man, 'let the fella deal. Do we have a choice?'

'N-no, we don't,' stuttered pale face. 'We don't have no choice. But if it's money—'

'Yuh got only one choice,' said Brown, ranging the Winchester again. 'Yuh get flat to the floor, every one of yuh, and yuh stay there. Yuh understand – *yuh stay there*. First to lift a head is dead as dirt. Now, douse them lights and do it!'

'Like the man says,' murmured Charlie. 'Just like the man says.'

Brown waited until the car was in darkness before blazing the Winchester's lead loose and wild to the ceiling.

'Where is he? Where that sonofa-snorin'-bitch go? Yuh see him?' Lud Reemer swung round, left then right, his Colt menacing and grim in his grip, his weight pushing Morgan Friar to one side. 'Yuh see him, damnit?' he snarled.

'Who?' croaked Friar, one eye on Reemer, the other watching the four men moving in a slow, silent line to the bulk of the main freight car. 'What the hell yuh talkin' about?'

'Fella back there in the corner seat. Boarded at the Junction.' Reemer ranged the Colt again. 'Supposed to be sleepin', but he weren't, nothin' like sleepin'. I seen types like him before. No good. No damn good at all. So where is he?'

'Couldn't give a spit. You just get y'self along of the boys there. Minute that freight door slides open—'

Reemer swung away, his gaze squinting to the darkness beyond the cars. 'Slipped away, ain't he?' he mouthed. 'Vanished. Don't trust fellas like that when they just disappear.'

'F'get it, will yuh?' said Friar, pulling at Reemer's shirt. 'We ain't here for wet nursin' the where-abouts of passengers. Case yuh overlooked it, we gotta shipment of gold here waitin' on us. Now get to it!'

Reemer eased back. 'That fella standin' to yuh, where'd yuh find him? Yuh checked him out? Yuh trust him?'

'Brown? Sure, I trust him. Dragged him outa the jail here. He'd have been stretched end of a rope by now if I hadn't. Brown's with us. Yuh can trust him.'

'Strangers ain't for easy trustin',' mouthed Reemer again, his gaze still probing the shadows, fingers working anxiously at the butt of the Colt. 'He in for a share?' he asked.

'What do you think?' drawled Friar.

'I think we got enough bodies in on this.'

'Precisely,' grinned Friar. 'Now, yuh goin' to get to that gold, or ain't yuh? And remember – no prisoners.' His stare hardened. 'Yuh leave the strangers to me.'

Reemer murmured a curse, spun the Colt through his fingers and turned to the line of men. 'Just watch for the sleepin' one, all right?'

Two figures bent low, moving softly, silently from the tumble of old shacks to the wagons drawn up in the thicker shadows far side of the rail head; pausing a moment, waiting, no sounds from them or between them; slipping on, pausing again, tensing at the crack of rifle shots, the sudden swish and grind of a freight car's door sliding open.

'What's that? What's goin' on there? They shootin' up the passengers?'

Bart Jessom's stare widened, bloodshot and watering. 'Yuh see that? Sonofa-goddamn-bitch!'

Joe Fane winced at the gunfire, blinked and swallowed, and was twitching in the chill of his sweat at the blurred reach of lantern light from the freight car as its doors opened fully and men appeared in the glow, hovered, hesitated in the confusion and noise, gazes swinging to left and right, probing the darkness, then began to fall one by one under the hail of Colt fire from the line of guns facing them.

'It's a hold-up!' he hissed. 'Hell, it's an all-time hold-up!'

'Bloody massacre!' croaked Bart, his throat suddenly tight and dry.

'The wagons,' hissed Joe again. 'That's what they're here for, damn it. Here for the getaway.'

'Let's do it, Joe. F'Cris'sake, let's do it!'

Two figures moving again, scurrying now through the dapplings of moonlight to the patches of shadow, edging closer to the wagons and the hitched teams beginning to fret, their eyes white, wide and bulging.

Joe concentrated on the wagon to his right, motioning for Bart to head to the left. They went low and fast, halting only once, flat in the dirt, at the echoing whine and blaze of more gunshots, voices, curses, Friar barking orders, and somewhere deep in the depths of the darkened passenger cars the soft sobbing of a girl.

'Don't wait, just do it,' mouthed Joe. 'Scatter the horses, then fire the wagons. Make for the shacks when it's done.'

Bart raised a hand and scurried on.

'World's goin' mad,' groaned Gus Smalley, turning from his cover in the debris of the livery as Lacy Alice ushered the bar girls from the shadows. 'And y'self right along of it,' he added with a slap of his lips. 'Hell, yuh got any idea at all what yuh doin'?'

'I know,' said Alice, 'and I ain't for waitin' on thinkin' it through. I got these guns here, I got ammunition, and I got the girls. Don't know a deal about guns, 'ceptin' they can sure as hell wreak havoc when yuh got a finger on the right bit, but I know my girls. So that's what we'll go and do – wreak havoc.'

'But Alice—' spluttered Gus.

'But nothin'. Still don't know what's goin' on out there, but it don't sound good. And if this town's goin' down, and us with it, might as well do it in style.' Alice tossed her loose hair into her neck. 'Well, yuh with us? Didn't go to all the trouble of gettin' these guns just to look at 'em, did yuh? 'Course yuh didn't. So grab that piece there and stand to us, Gus

Smalley. Right now, while there's still a spark of decency left in yuh.'

She swung round to the night beyond the ruins. 'More to the point, while we're still breathin',' she murmured.

SEVENTEEN

'Stand back there, all of yuh. Stand back!' Morgan Friar's order cracked like a whip as he shouldered a path through his sidekicks, picked his way between the crumpled bodies of the shipment guards and stared into the gaping space of the freight car.

'Yeah . . .' he mouthed softly, his eyes glinting in the smoke-wisped darkness, 'all a man could ever want. Right here. Simple as pickin' cherries.' He flexed his shoulders, broke the reverie, and turned to Reemer. 'Bring up the wagons. We load smartish, finish here and get clear.' His gaze narrowed. 'Yuh hearin' me there, Lud? Yuh heard a word of what I been sayin'?'

'I hear yuh,' drawled the man, dragging his stare from the shadows.

'Well, try lookin' as if yuh had, f'Cris'sake!' Friar stepped back from the car. 'Yuh ain't still frettin' on that stranger, are yuh? He still fidgetin' at yuh?'

'Where'd he go, that's what I wanna know? Where'd the sonofabitch bury himself? Fella like that don't just vanish. T'ain't natural.'

'Damnit, we got gold here fellas would die for, and

104

all you can do is pick over some scumbag drifter! Yuh just get to clearin' these bodies here, get them wagons pulled up. Let's put this town back of us!'

'Where's that fella Brown?' croaked Reemer.

'Settlin' them first-class passengers. Yuh heard the shots.'

'I heard four shots,' said Reemer, raising a crooked eyebrow. 'And that's all I heard.'

Friar's lips tightened to a cracked, narrow line. 'Just get to doin' what we're here for, Lud,' he hissed. 'Do it – before yuh get to bein' an itch I might be real tempted to scratch!'

He turned to the others waiting in the darkness. 'Yuh did a good job here, boys. Clean and fast, just the way I like it. So now we get to the good part, eh? Load up, hit the Sands and have ourselves a share-out. That suit yuh?' The men shuffled and murmured. 'Fine. And remember, dead folk don't talk, so we don't leave nobody breathin'. Not one.'

'What about the folk in town?' asked a hooded-eyed man from the back of the group. 'They seen us.'

'I ain't fussed none about them,' grinned Friar. 'Ain't worth a husk. Not one of 'em moved a finger against us, have they? Not a muscle. I got this town right where I want it, just like I said I would. Ain't that so?'

The men might have agreed, might have stepped then to the crates in the freight car and got to the business of stacking a fortune in readiness for the wagons. Lud Reemer might have dismissed the shadows and the missing stranger. Gold and the prospect of it had its lure, and when it was right there, just waiting on a fellow helping himself. . . .

But the next sound to come from that gathering of

men at the silent, blood-smeared rail head was a pitched curse, a scuffing of anxious boots across boards, more curses, groans, as the men turned bewildered gazes to the sight of the wagons engulfed in a raging blaze of flames and the teams scattering in the jangle of loose, trailing tack to the night.

Lud Reemer was the first to move, slowly with barely a breath escaping him, his gaze suddenly dark and piercing as he turned once again to the shadows behind him.

Charlie Hicks spat the dust from his mouth, ran his tongue over his uneven teeth, the tricklings of sweat at his lips, and shifted himself a fraction higher from his cramped position behind the first-class seat.

Flames – a whole licking rush of them, right there, somewhere among the old shacks, mirrored in the car window as if someone had torched the night. Hell, just what in the name of sanity was happening out there?

'Lord in Heaven, where are we now?' groaned a voice behind him.

'Some party,' murmured the gambling man.

'When my boys get to hearin' of this . . .' croaked the Bar Nine cattle king.

'Oh, do stop snivellin', Letitia,' tutted the colonel's wife through a haze of lavender scent.

The girl sniffed loudly and sobbed again.

'Why don't they just take the money?' muttered the man with the canvas valise from somewhere deep in a shadowed corner. 'I got money. Any amount.'

Charlie spat again and risked another move.

'Fella could've killed us all, so how come he didn't?' came a voice from the far end of the

compartment. 'What he was here for, weren't it? So
how come? Answer me that.'

'Who's askin?' hissed another voice. 'Just do as the
fella said: stay low, f'Cris'sake – beggin' yuh pardon,
ladies.'

'Stay here and fry!' snapped the gambler. 'Yuh see
them flames out there? See 'em? Another few
minutes and we'll all be ash.'

'Don't nobody move,' snapped Charlie. 'We're
breathin', ain't we? Fella didn't kill us, did he?'

'So where'd he go?' hissed the hotel proprietor.
'What's to stop us leavin' right now?'

'Hot lead,' drawled a voice. 'Yuh fancy it, it's
waitin' on yuh.'

'Hold it,' said Charlie, easing still higher. 'This is
rail company business – *my* business. So don't nobody
move 'til I say so, yuh hear?'

The girl sobbed, the woman tutted, the proprietor
sighed, and the pale-faced man hugged the valise to
him as if it were a child.

It took Charlie Hicks another full minute to find
his feet and edge carefully towards the compartment
door. The man with the Winchester was not to be
seen.

But where, he wondered, was the corner seat,
sleeping marshal?

'Get them doors closed!' bellowed Friar, spinning on
his heel from the rage of flaming wagons. 'Get 'em
closed. Seal that car tight!'

'Got the town in yuh grip, eh?' drawled Reemer
through a twisted, cynical grin. 'Looks that way, don't
it?'

'Shut yuh mouth!' Friar's gaze swung wildly

among the sidekicks as they heaved on the freight car doors. 'Go check out that passenger car. Get a hold of the engineer drivin' this heap.'

'What yuh plannin'?'

'Takin' the train, ain't I?' said Friar, spinning again to face Reemer, a grin twitching at the corners of his mouth. 'Who needs wagons when we gotta train waitin' on us? Simple – we fuel up and steam the whole caboodle down the line. Some place remote 'til we get sorted again. Get ourselves new wagons, head south. . . . Hell, that's just detail! There's a fortune in our hands and we ain't losin' it, so why don't yuh get yuh butt shiftin', f'Cris'sake, 'stead of standin' there like some dimwit drifter?' He turned back to the sidekicks. 'Seal it, damn yuh!'

The doors clanged shut with a shuddering thud, the flaming wagons lit the high night sky, sweeping deep shadows across the huddle of old shacks, the silent, staring clusters of dazed townfolk, too scared and fuddle-headed to do more than just stand there like strangers to a time and place.

'Yuh all through there?' shouted Friar, spinning his Colt through his fingers.

'All through, Mr Friar,' called a sidekick.

'Good. Now yuh listen up, all of yuh.' The man strode a few measured paces over the boards, glared at the burning wagons, the dark silhouetted shapes of the town, spun the Colt on the flickering light, and turned to face the men. 'Change of plan. Seems like we got some maverick scumbags back there in town. Gettin' themselves fire happy! Well, t'ain't no sweat. Made their point and I hope they feel the better for it.' Friar spun the Colt again, spat across the barrel and rubbed his fingers through the spittle. 'First one shows a limb this side of the rail head gets it split along with the rest of his mangy body. No foolin'!'

The men murmured and nodded. 'Mebbe we should get to showin' 'em a real blaze, eh?' drawled one. 'Put their whole damned town to the torch!'

'And mebbe we will at that,' grinned Friar, raising an arm to silence the group. 'Sure we will, but right now we got other concerns. Gold concerns – that right? Well, yuh bet on it, boys! Now we ain't got the time to go searchin' out new wagons, not here, anyhow. So we take the train, all of it, every last nut and goddamn bolt! Yuh hear that?'

The men shouted their agreement.

'So let's get to it! We steam up, pull out down the line, ten, twenty miles or so, then—'

'Not so fast there.'

Friar and the gathering turned as one to the deeper shadows, the snap of the voice, the blurred movement as figures approached: Reemer, Colt drawn in one hand, the other vice-like in its grip on Brown's arm twisted high into his shoulder-blades.

'Yuh want for me to finish him now?' scowled the sidekick, levelling the gun at Brown's temple. ''Cus I sure as hell should. Oh, yes, that I certainly should.' He tightened the grip and twisted the arm until Brown's face creased with the pain. 'He ain't shot no passengers. Nothin' like. They're alive, every one of 'em. Found this scum skulkin' round the engine.'

Friar's Colt was suddenly still and heavy in his hand, his face pale in the mottled darkness.

'Know what I figure?' growled Reemer. 'This fella ain't nobody worth a peck of dirt. Yellow-livered with it. So how come he's here in Peaceway, eh? Gamblin' type, yuh say – the hell he is!'

'Yuh disappoint me, Mr Brown,' said Friar, licking at a trickle of sweat in the corner of his mouth. 'Reckoned yuh for a whole lot smarter, 'specially after all I done for yuh and you lookin' to me like yuh did along of Hendy back there.' He sighed and wiped the barrel of the Colt across the front of his shirt. 'Yuh goin' to tell me about it?'

'We ain't got the time,' spat Reemer impatiently, thrusting at another twist. 'Finish it now.'

'Yuh told 'em about the marshal?' groaned Brown, wincing against the hold. 'Bet yuh ain't at that.'

'Marshal?' clipped Reemer. 'What marshal? What's he on about?'

'T'ain't nothin',' huffed Friar.

'Quaid,' groaned Brown again. 'Yuh got Marshal Quaid—'

A hiss and spit of steam rushed like a shivering shroud across the night, a clang and spinning of wheels pierced the silence that was filled in the seconds that followed by the shuddering roar and heave of Engine 37 grinding into a lunge forward.

'What the hell . . ?' growled Reemer, dragging Brown with him in his spin.

'The engine, f'Cris'sake!' yelled a sidekick. 'It's pullin' out!'

'Somebody's uncoupled it!' shouted another.

'Sonofa—'

But Reemer's growling, gurgling curse was lost somewhere in the depths of his throat as 37's whistle shrieked across the night, its wheels spinning, pistons wheezing, thrusting the locomotive into a charging surge down the line, the headlight blazing like a frenzied eye.

It was disappearing in a cloud of smoke and sparks

when Reemer's finger on the trigger of his Colt lost control and blew a hole deep in the gambling man's head.

Brown's last breath was lost in the echo of 37's departing shriek.

EIGHTEEN

They slipped softly, silently, some of them on tiptoe, through the empty shadows of the alley at the back of the saloon, paused in the cover of the crates and waited for the signal. Nobody murmured, nobody moved, save to shift their wide-eyed gazes over the night. One of them shivered, another put a shaking hand to trembling lips.

Gus Smalley hissed for silence and peered into the sprawl of the old shacks. Had to be somebody out there, had to be. Teams were not for slipping free of wagons of their own accord, and only a human hand got to torching outfits that way. And just whose hand was it had uncoupled 37 from the cars and freight wagons? He swallowed and screwed his eyes against the bite of the dryness. Hell, all this was getting beyond him. No saying what might happen.

'They ain't goin' no place, are they?' whispered Lacy Alice. 'No wagons, no engine.' She half turned to urge the bar girls to total silence, then flicked a hand for Gus to join her. 'I figure for the torchin' bein' the work of Joe and Bart. What yuh reckon?'

'Could be,' murmured Gus. 'But, damnit, Alice,

112

what's the difference? This ain't for us, is it? Scum like them at the train there ain't for tanglin' with. Yuh can see what they done already: taken out the fellas in that freight car like they were swattin' flies. And I ain't mistaken none, am I, that is Brown lyin' there, dead as dirt, ain't it?' He swallowed again. 'No, this ain't for us. Best we can do is get ourselves hid somewhere till it's over.'

'No way!' snapped Alice. 'I ain't lettin' the likes of Friar get away with this. 'Sides, there's passengers out there. See that – light in first-class. We can't just turn our backs, can we? Folk there need some help.'

'Sure,' gulped Gus. 'But a handful of bar gals who wouldn't know a barrel from a butt when it comes to guns ain't exactly scarin', is it?'

Alice tossed her hair defiantly. 'We're movin' in, close as we can get. That last shack there. All right? And you, mister, can get to thinkin' straight. Go see if yuh can find Bart and Joe; round up the townfolk, get 'em organized some place. Mahooney's bar. And if there's anybody – *anybody* – fit enough and minded enough to lend a hand to us, grab 'em before they change their mind! Yuh got that?' Her eyes glinted in the moonlight. 'Oh, and Gus, keep a watch for that marshal fella.'

'Marshal?' frowned Gus. 'Yuh mean Quaid? F'get it, Alice, he ain't here and he ain't never goin' to be. Know what, I don't think Marshal Quaid ever was plannin' on bein' here. Best we got on that count is the ghost of him, just like we're goin' to finish up with a ghost town here. And mebbe we deserve it.'

Alice hugged herself against the chill and eased her gaze back to what remained of the night train. Looked awful ghostly standing there, she thought.

*

Charlie Hicks flexed his shoulders against the sticky damp of his shirt and stared through the half-lit gloom of the first-class car into Morgan Friar's face.

Fellow was lathering himself up some and watching that sidekick along him like he was a diseased dog. Who was trusting to who here, and how long before the whole simmering pot of it boiled over? Hell, he should have seen this coming, should have figured the five scum riding second-class for what they were; and should have known sure as day to night that a freight car of Western and Central gold was never going to be an easy ride.

He squirmed, swallowed and stifled a wince at the twist of pain in his gut. The bank guards had died almost before they had seen the faces of their killers, minute the wagon doors had opened and they had blinked on the shadowed gloom of Peaceway. One breath of that sultry night air. . . . And it had been their last.

He winced again. Gunning men down like that, as cold-blooded and nerveless as stepping on dazed flies, had been the far side of Hell. Somebody would have to pay, somehow, somewhere. . . . But right now, way that fellow Friar was jumping, his sidekick there twitching, just about anybody might be next for that Hell, in the same loose-handed way they had shot the fellow with the Winchester.

Even so, thought Charlie, somebody had uncoupled 37 and Taffs had been there to drive it clear. Only person he could reckon for doing that had to be the fellow in the corner seat. But just where, damn it, was he?

'Yuh knew, didn't yuh?' growled Reemer, his glare scorching Charlie's face. 'The sleeper – he tell yuh he was Quaid? Sure he did. So what else he tell yuh?'

'Nothin',' fumbled Charlie. 'Didn't say nothin'.'

'Good mind to whip every word outa yuh right now,' growled Reemer. 'Whip yuh till there ain't—'

'You will hang!' said the colonel's wife, one hand fluttering to her daughter's shoulder. 'My husband will personally ensure you do.'

'If it's money yuh want,' began the pale-faced man, offering the valise.

'Strikes me they got all they want somewhere back there,' mouthed the gambler. 'What the hell we haulin' here, anyhow?'

'Gold,' groaned Charlie. ' 'Bout as much as a fella's ever likely to see.'

'Well, gold don't fuss me none,' huffed the cattleman. 'Don't set no store to it, so mebbe we should get to talkin' serious here. Now, way I see it—'

'Shut it!' spat Friar, turning his Colt through his fingers. 'Next one opens his mouth, it stays that way.' He drew Reemer to the far end of the car. 'We gotta plan some,' he murmured quickly.

'Yuh should've done some plannin' way back!' drawled Reemer. 'How long yuh known about Quaid, f'Cris'sake? Been a year since you and him last tangled, so how come he's here?'

'I didn't know 'til I hit town, swear to God I didn't.'

'Well, yuh sure as hell know now, don't yuh?' sneered Reemer. 'And he's a real problem, ain't he? Oh, yes, a real thorn in yuh boot.'

'Mebbe, but we got an edge here. We got the passengers. Good as money in the bank.'

'What yuh sayin?' frowned Reemer.

'I'm talkin' hostages. Quaid ain't goin' to move
against the threat of us killin' these folk one by one,
is he? T'ain't in his moralizin' law book. No, he'll
stand off. Have to. No choice while we get ourselves
new wagons and load up.'

'And just where yuh goin' to get new wagons? And
while you're at it, answer me this: just who was that
fella Brown?'

'Yuh got a twisted mind there, Lud,' grinned Friar.
'Darn sight too fretful and fidgetin', yuh know that?
Hell, we got guns and men and a train here full of
folk ready to trade their souls to stay breathin' – *and*
we got that town out there. So there's a bothersome
marshal on the loose. So? He's one man, ain't he?
Just one man.'

'Tell that to the last fella he dragged to his
hangin',' said Reemer, his gaze filling with a sudden
shift of shadows.

It would never work – worse, it just might! But if it
did and he was still alive to see it, what then? State of
the minds of the scum back there, and with that
amount of gold at stake, there might be nobody left
to tell it and damn all of a town still standing.

Charlie Hicks walked on; slow, measured, careful
steps, same pace, straight line – straight as his shaking knees would permit – the white cloth loose in his
hand, the sweat trickling into his neck, his gaze
swinging left to right, then hovering like a beam,
Friar's words still echoing in his head:

'Yuh get that conductor's cap on yuh head and
yuh get out there, show them dumb townfolk a flag
of truce and start negotiating, yuh hear? And here's
what yuh tell 'em: yuh say as how I want that under-

taker fella, name of Charlie Copps, to get his hearse hitched and here in an hour. And no excuses. If he ain't got a team to haul it, he finds one. Double quick! One hour.'

Friar had stepped carefully through the shadows of the car to face the colonel's snivelling daughter, his gaze ice-cold behind the gleam of sweat. 'And if he don't do exactly that, we start puttin' these good folk outa their misery, one by one, with the girl here last – when Reemer and the boys have seen a sight more of what she's hidin' 'neath them satin skirts. I make m'self clear? Yuh understand? So do it!'

Charlie swallowed, hesitated a moment, the cloth sad and shaking in his hand, his eyes blurred now in the strain of watching and peering.

Almost into the main street; light there in the saloon; rest of the place in darkness, silent, nobody moving, waiting, leastways not that he could see. Hell, might be anybody in any one of the black alleys, the shadows, blind, faceless windows. Might be somebody with a gun and in no mood for paying regard to a rail conductor and a white flag. Might be somebody too scared to pay regard to anything save survival.

But the town was not deserted. Nothing like. He could feel it; a presence, perhaps a face, eyes, an itchy finger, somebody not thinking straight. Who was? Who could? The silence was saying it all. Night such as this had been. . . .

A shape there, somebody moving, easing from the depths of shadow like a black beetle.

'Hold it right there, mister. Not another step.'

A woman's voice, dry and clipped, sharp as needles, not for messing. Figure stepping into the street now, handful of bar girls following her. Too right there would be no messing, thought Charlie, coming to a clumsy, shuffling halt. Woman and the girls were armed – and not for decoration!

'I see yuh, I see yuh,' he stuttered, gulping on the pinch in his throat. 'Just go easy, will yuh, and hear me out? I gotta message from them scum back there at the train, and it ain't good. Yuh gotta hear me.'

'We're listenin',' said Lacy Alice, moving into the street. 'Make it quick. Time's pressin'.'

'You bet it is, lady. A whole lot more than yuh think.' He gulped again. 'Yuh got an undertaker hereabouts, name of Copps? Yuh'd better have. There's business waitin' on him. And it's a whole sight more than dead bodies!'

NINETEEN

'Yuh see that? Flag of truce. Just what in hell's that fella Friar plannin' now?' Joe Fane gestured through the shadows for Bart Jessom to slip closer through the mounds of crates, boxes and loose timbers in the rail head loading bay. 'What yuh reckon?' he whispered.

'All goin' wrong, ain't it?' said Bart, wiping a hand across his sticky, smoke- and smut-smeared face. 'We set a whole crowd of hornets buzzin'.' A soft, satisfied smile flickered at his lips. 'No wagons, no engine. . . . Some mess. Tell yuh somethin', though, t'ain't so good for them passengers there. Hell, no. Wouldn't give them gunslingin' vermin an inch of dirt.'

'So mebbe we should get busy again, eh?' grinned Joe. 'Give 'em all somethin' to keep 'em busy. What yuh say? Another torchin'?'

'I say we get back into town. Get to Alice, the girls, find out what that white flag means. Too many guns here to my likin'. We done enough. Don't let's push our luck.'

'Luck ain't in it, Bart,' hissed Joe. 'We're gettin' an edge here, ain't we? Doin' somethin' decent for once. Don't let's get to paddlin' wet feet when we got the chance—'

Bart's hand fell in an iron grip to Joe's arm as he grunted a warning and nodded to the reach of the deeper darkness beyond the rail track. 'Just who the devil's that?'

Joe raised himself higher, narrowed his eyes and peered at the figure of the man, tall and straight, broad-shouldered, easy stance in his weight to one leg, the folds of his frock coat drawn clear on his right where the Peacemaker Colt hung to its holster; wide-brimmed hat tipped low, clean shirt, polished boots and nothing about him seeming to move, save for the slow curl of cheroot smoke from his lips and the gaze that sidled over the night like the stinging gleam of a rattler's stare.

'That who I think it might be?' croaked Bart.

'Marshal Quaid, sure as day,' said Joe, still peering. 'How the hell he get here?'

'On the train. Only way.' Bart swallowed. 'Some look in his eyes there . . . sonofa-goddamn-bitch, ain't there just. Wouldn't fancy for them settlin' my way.' He swallowed again, louder and deeper. 'Know somethin', Joe, we should get back to town right now, this minute. We're no match for what's comin' up here.'

'Yeah,' mouthed Joe vaguely, his eyes widening on the figure in the dark, 'yuh right, dead right, and I would too, Bart, get the hell out of it along of yuh, savin' that we can't. We ain't goin' no place. He's seen us!'

Lacy Alice turned on her heels from the batwings of Mahooney's bar, flounced her skirts, tossed her hair

and stared deep into Charlie Hicks's creased, lathered face.

'Yuh could use a drink there, mister,' she said
through a tight half smile. 'Gus, give Mr Hicks a shot
of the best. Back counter, bottom shelf.'

'Well, mebbe I will at that,' trembled Charlie,
mopping his face with the white cloth. 'Don't
normally, not when I'm on duty. But, heck, I guess
this is a mite beyond the call of duty.'

'I'd reckon,' said Alice. 'Just one, mark yuh. I want
yuh back on that train sober as a struttin' rooster.'
She crossed to the bar, leaned against it, glanced
quickly at the girls gathered in the far corner, and
traced a finger through the dregs of a spilled drink.
'So yuh got it all clear in yuh mind?' she began again,
watching Charlie savour his shot. 'Yuh know exactly
what to tell Friar?'

'I know. I got it,' said Charlie, swallowing noisily.
'Hearse'll be there in an hour, Copps drivin' it.' He
finished the drink. 'Friar'll buy that.'

'He'd better,' said Alice, ' 'cus it's all we got for
now.' The tracing finger halted, then moved through
a slow, careful circle. 'Yuh sure yuh ain't seen nothin'
of that marshal since the train pulled in?' she asked,
raising an eyebrow.

'Nothin',' sighed Charlie, mopping at his face
again. 'Just melted away. But tell yuh somethin', he
ain't gone far. He's waitin' some place. Quiet type,
yuh know? Don't fuss none, but don't scare easy
neither.' He lowered the cloth from his gleaming
face. 'Yep, he's out there. Just wish he'd get to whatever he's a mind for. Friar'll wanna be clear of town
come first light.'

'And Brown?' asked Alice quietly.

'Dead,' said Charlie, lowering his gaze to the cloth. 'Did his best for the passengers; should've shot 'em, but he didn't – the hell he didn't! Tell yuh another thing, it was him and the engineer uncoupled old 37. So why'd he do that? Couldn't have been standin' that close to Friar, could he? No way.'

'All that gold . . .' murmured Gus from behind the bar, his grip on a bottle forgotten. 'Think of what Hendy would've done for a sight of it. Hell, Peaceway folk never figured for nothin' like this.'

'And might not be around to tell it!' snapped Alice. 'So let's move shall we? Gus, yuh know what to do. Girls, yuh stay outa sight and don't stray none. And you, Mr Hicks, had best get to that train before Friar starts frettin' on them passengers. Follow me. We'll use the back way.'

Alice had led Charlie through the shadowed alley at the rear of the saloon, between the maze of crates and barrels to the fringe of the sprawl of the old shacks, assured him again of all the help she could summon and watched him stumble his way back to the rail head and the waiting line of cars, when she turned with the notion of heading for the funeral parlour to make her plans with Copps.

No telling if what she had in mind would work – no telling, come to that, if the nervy-eyed undertaker would go along with it, but somebody had to do something to give the passengers a chance. Friar would not be for leaving witnesses. He would be for a clean, no clutter getaway; nobody stacking up memories back of their minds, nobody left to recall faces, snatches of conversation, and maybe nothing of Peaceway worth the picking over.

Friar had too much at stake – a fortune and his life.

Even so, she thought, threading her way through the jumble of crates and shadows, he had not reckoned on Quaid, on him being aboard the train – and not by chance neither – and maybe he had read that fellow Brown all wrong. And if he had, maybe that would confirm. . . .

But Alice's thoughts had been stifled right there where she stood in the deepest of the darkness, one hand feeling for the edge of a crate, one foot a step from a barrel, the glow of the soft light from the bar beyond her in the deserted street, the silence like a shroud, the night chill feeling for her.

Had it been the drift of smoke, the smell of it, the merest scuff of a boot at the dirt, or perhaps the half of a shadow that moved, or perhaps she had seen the eyes?

She would never be sure, only conscious of her sharp, stabbing intake of breath and the shiver that began somewhere in her neck, and then of waiting for the sound of the voice.

'Been a while, Alice. Yuh lookin' good.'

She had wanted to speak, but her mouth had stayed closed, tight against the dryness in her throat; wanted to blink, but felt only the prickle of the sweat on her brow.

'Bad business we got here,' came the voice again. 'Sorry yuh got caught in it.'

Alice fought back the tremble of another shiver and swallowed deeply. 'Quaid,' she croaked. 'Yuh made it.'

'Yeah,' sighed the man, the gleam in his eyes shading for a moment. 'But not soon enough, 'specially for some. Lost me a good man t'night. The best.'

'Brown?' gulped Alice. 'One of your men?'

'Deputy these past three years.'

'Hell!' Alice eased a slow step forward. 'Yuh had this all set, the whole thing. Brown bein' here. . . . Yuh knew Friar was plannin' the raid. . . . Yuh used Hendy. . . . Hell!' She wiped a hand across her neck and into the fall of her hair. 'But it ain't quite worked, has it? There's men died out there t'night. There's them passengers. . . . There's *us*, right here, damn it!'

'Yuh readin' it right, but it ain't over, not yet it ain't,' said Quaid, dropping the butt of a cheroot to the dirt and heeling it. 'Plannin' don't always go yuh way. There's a cost when it don't, the highest when it happens a good man loses his life. Now it's time to finish it. Payback time on more than one count.'

'On yuh own, here, in this place, with about as much goin' for yuh as a fly in a flood?' Alice tossed her hair and licked at the cold sweat on her lip. 'I seen the fella in action back of that law mask yuh wear. I seen him . . . the Falls, Coppertown, River Hand. . . . Reputation goes ahead of yuh. But I'm tellin' yuh, Marshal, this time, in Peaceway, with that sonofabitch Friar waitin' on yuh, hell, yuh got any sorta chance?'

Quaid's eyes settled in a tight stare. 'Pair of us might just see this through,' he murmured. 'What yuh reckon?'

Only then did Lacy Alice's shoulders ease from their tension as the night air chilled and she surrendered to a long, deep shiver.

TWENTY

Lud Reemer shifted his weight against the jamb of the door at the far end of the first-class compartment and swung his gaze slowly over the sweating faces of the staring passengers.

Nothing to be said for any one of them, he thought, with a sniff: racy gamblers, paunchy cattle baron, frilly woman and her snivelling daughter, shifty-eyed hotel type, fellow with the valise . . . not a peck of fight among them, saving maybe the frilly woman. She might get to mouthing some when the time came.

He shifted again and half turned to peer through the open door to the night. Whole lot different out there. More fight than a fellow might want to handle, and all down to one man – the sleeper in the corner seat, Marshal Quaid. Get to tangling with a fellow like that and you were wrestling a bad-tempered rattler. Heard it said a hundred times through a dozen territories. Heard Friar himself say as much: '*Yuh get a glimpse of Quaid, yuh stay with him. Don't never blink.*'

And Friar should know, better than most. Written across his face right now, standing there on the platform. He might look to be waiting on the return of the conductor, but two-bits to a pocket of dirt there was a whole buzz of doubt plaguing him. A freight car of gold there for the taking, but the shape of Quaid in every shadow. No time for blinking.

'Yuh see him?' asked Reemer, moving to Friar's side.

'He'll be here,' murmured Friar, his gaze deep on the night.

'That Quaid or the conductor yuh referrin' to?'

'Quaid don't fuss me none, not here, not with the guns we got. Fella ain't that stupid.'

'So yuh figure for him just ridin' out soon as he gets himself a horse? Leave us to help ourselves, finish them passengers minute they ain't of no value, get to one helluva share-out. . . . Oh, sure, Marshal Quaid's that generous, ain't he? Real considerate fella!'

Friar turned, tense and fiery eyed. 'He really bugs yuh some, don't he? Got himself squirmin' under yuh skin.'

'Could be you're the one squirmin', Morgan,' sneered Reemer. 'Could be this is what yuh been sweatin' on all these years – a showdown with Quaid. Hell, fella's been sittin' on yuh tail for long enough. Yuh reckon on him lettin' go now, this close?' He aimed a line of spittle to the platform boards. 'Yuh never figured for this, did yuh? No how. And sorta ironic, ain't it, him waitin' on yuh, any one of them shadows, just when yuh got yuh fingers near as damnit on yuh biggest haul yet?'

Reemer's eyes darkened. 'He must've known yuh'd be here. Must've been plannin' this every step of the way, sittin' right there at yuh back, watchin' every move, *knowin'* it – just like he is now.'

'Yuh that wound up about the fella, why don't you go take care of him?' hissed Friar, a line of sweat trickling from his hatband. 'Or mebbe he's a heap too much for yuh.'

'And mebbe I will at that,' said Reemer, his fingers tapping over the butt of his Colt. 'I got an investment here, big as it comes, so mebbe I should look to it.' A soft grin slid across his lips. 'Seems like somebody's got to, don't it?'

Friar's gaze moved back to the night. 'Suit y'self. I got my own business.'

Lud Reemer spat again and wandered slowly towards the loading bay. Should never have taken his eyes off that fellow in the corner seat, he mused, not for a second.

Not even to blink.

Joe Fane slid his thumbs over the loose drag of his braces and hissed through his teeth for Bart Jessom's attention. 'See that?' he mouthed softly. 'See that scumbag there, headin' this way? One of Friar's guns. Mebbe we should try takin' him out, eh? What yuh reckon?'

Bart blinked and gulped on a gravel-chip throat. 'Yuh outa your head, or somethin'?' he moaned, his fingers settling like claws on the knotty edges of a wooden crate. 'Yuh get to within a spit of a fella like that and he'd blow yuh head before yuh'd taken breath.' He gulped again and ran his tongue to the sticky corners of his mouth. 'Leave it, Joe, just leave it. We know what we gotta do. Marshal spelled it out clear enough, didn't he? Said as how we were to go help them passengers soon as Friar and his boys make a move. And that's it – that's just what we'll do. I ain't for crossin' Quaid.'

'Yeah, yeah, I hear yuh,' sighed Joe on a whisper. 'Just don't take none to them vermin struttin' about like that. Just wanna get to doin' somethin', f'Cris'sake.'

'Done enough for now to my reckonin',' trembled Bart, his fingers digging deeper. 'Gettin' m'self tied in with Hendy, puttin' a gun in the fella's hands, damn it, and then seein' that fella Brown go down like he did, bein' here and still breathin'. . . . Hell, Joe, best thing that's happened is Quaid spottin' us. Least we can do now is go along with him.'

Joe turned a slow, measured gaze to Bart's sweating face. 'Yuh figure for him settlin' this?' he murmured. 'One man, on his own?'

'Yuh see his eyes?' asked Bart. 'Damn it, yuh stood here lookin' at him, hearin' him, yuh seen that look same as I did. Anybody goin' to sort this, it'll be Quaid, which is why we gotta do as he asked – get to them passengers when the times comes.'

Joe hitched his braces and eased lower into the shadows behind the crates. 'So where'd yuh reckon that scum's goin?' he whispered, nodding to the dark shape of the figure moving towards the old shacks. 'He ain't stretchin' his legs for his health, is he?'

'Might be stretchin' 'em a step too far if he's headin' where I think he is.'

'Lookin' for Quaid?'

'Lookin' is mebbe all he will do.'

The Bar Nine cattleman tugged at the neck of his shirt, tore it open and slapped a fat-fingered hand over the lathering of sweat on the hairs of his chest. 'Well, we just goin' to wait here?' he wheezed. 'We goin' to get to doin' somethin', f'Cris'sake?'

The colonel's wife dabbed at the dust on the folds of her dress, glared at her wet-eyed daughter and stiffened her shoulders. 'And what precisely are you suggesting we do?' she asked, her neck growing out of her buttoned blouse like a stalk. 'The only *doing* is to stay alive. When my husband—'

'He ain't here, lady, and ain't likely to be,' said a gambler, bending to peer through a compartment window. 'And if we get to seein' anythin' of sun-up out there it'll be a miracle.'

'Any sign of that conductor?' muttered the hotel proprietor. 'What's keepin' him?'

'Well, he ain't takin' no stroll, is he?' mocked the second gambler, stretching his hand to finger a signet ring.

'Damn it, we could put up some sorta fight,' snapped the cattleman. 'T'ain't in my nature to let filth like them fellas get away with this. Bar Nine boys'd been fightin' hell-for-leather. Wouldn't have seen the sweat for the blood!'

'Oh sure,' said the gambler, 'real rabble-rousin', spit-lickin' boys, eh? I'll bet! Only difference bein' they'd have the slight advantage of bein' armed.' He cocked a bushy eyebrow. 'Guns, mister, guns. Make one helluva difference, yuh know. And I don't see a piece between us, not one. All honest, peace-lovin' folk, ain't we?'

'Ain't fired a gun since I was a youth back home in Kansas,' muttered his colleague.

'Yuh ain't done nothin' since Kansas save bed whores and deal cards!'

'Really!' squeaked the colonel's wife. 'Is that necessary?'

The snivelling girl sniffed and widened her eyes.

'Close your ears, Letitia! Such talk!'

'Fact of life, ma'am,' grinned the gambler. 'Why, I recall one night back at Kneebend when this fella here had himself—'

'This ain't gettin' us nowhere,' growled the cattleman.

'Supposin' we make a run for it,' said the proprietor. 'Sneak outa here somehow.'

'*Sneak*, for God's sake,' laughed the gambler. 'Mister, yuh wouldn't get two steps before them scumbags riddled yuh. They ain't yuh average fellas out there, yuh know. They're killers, all through, and there's gold waitin' on 'em. *Gold*. Man ain't sane when there's gold at stake. I know, I seen it.'

'Well, mebbe, but that ain't to say we shouldn't try. Town looks quiet enough. Ain't nobody movin', hardly a light. We slip away now—'

'Wouldn't work,' clipped the cattleman. 'See us the minute we moved. No, we gotta fight, stand our ground. Win it, damn it! Same as me and the boys did out the Bonnet – fought for every inch of that goddamn dirt. Bar Nine weren't handed out on no plate. We made it ours! Sweat and blood of our hands. . . .'

'I don't want nobody rapin' me, not here I don't,' snivelled the girl.

'Letitia!'

The gambler burnished the ring on his jacket lapel, the proprietor licked his lips nervously, the cattleman wiped the sweat from his chest, the gambling man's colleague bent back to the window, and the pale-faced man clutching the valise came slowly, shakily to his feet in the shadowed corner.

'I gotta gun,' he stuttered. 'Sure I have. Right here. In my bag.'

TWENTY-ONE

Short steps and the grind of wheels to madness; only way to see it, thought Gus Smalley, wiping a hot, twitching hand through the dusty creases of his pants as he watched Charlie Copps drive the hearse from the dark depths of the funeral parlour to the deserted main street.

Anybody fool enough to reckon this for working had to be wild-eyed crazy. All Hendy's fault, he reckoned. Years of living under the heel of his boot had warped the minds of the townfolk, got them to a pitch where anything seemed possible, even reasonable. Even this! And Lacy Alice right there at the head of it, damn it. Last anybody might get to seeing of her again.

His hand twitched to a sweaty grip as the hearse slowed and came to a halt in the shadows short of the glow of light from the bar.

'Yuh all set there, Gus?' said Alice, easing one of the hearse drapes aside to peer out. 'Give us fifteen minutes, then y'self and Beanstalk follow through. Got it?'

'I got it,' croaked Gus. 'But, hell, Alice, yuh ain't never goin' to pull this off. Get y'self and the gals

132

there shot to pieces sure as fate. Minute yuh draw them drapes and Friar sees yuh all huddled back there—'

'Just yuh do your bit, Gus, and leave this to us.'

'But, Alice—'

'But nothin', there ain't the time.'

'What about Quaid?'

'What about him? Take care of himself, can't he?'

'*He* can,' groaned Gus. 'I ain't so certain about you. Them gals there ain't never pulled a trigger in their lives, and don't yuh go figurin' for Friar havin' qualms about shootin' up a hearse full of women. He'll do it, sure as hell he will.' He gulped. 'What a hearse is for, ain't it? Dead bodies!'

'Yuh soundin' like a frettin' woman there, Gus! Move on, Charlie, don't wanna keep them gold snatchers waitin'.'

Gus sighed, closed his eyes and shook his head as the hearse pulled away with all the solemn pace and dignity of a journey to Boot Hill.

And maybe it was just that, he thought.

Lud Reemer swept a slow, unblinking gaze over the high drift of the skies to the east. Softest touch of first light there, he reckoned. Night shadows would soon be trickling to grey, folk brave enough, or curious enough, in this morbid town beginning to move, eyes getting to see things.

Dangerous time, he mused; most anything could happen, catching a fellow unawares, specially so after a busy night and no sleep and the nerves got to dragging their heels. Paid to take a mite more extra care from here on, stay awake, keep moving, tight in the steps of the shifting shadows.

He waited a moment, easing his shoulders against the nip of the chill, tapped the butt of his holstered Colt, and slid away from the cover of the last of the old shacks.

So Friar figured for having this town buttoned down, did he, reckoned for it being too cold-sweat scared to move? Light there in the saloon bar told clear enough as how somebody was still about and not too minded about it being known. No saying how many along of him. No telling either what they were planning, or just who might be planning it.

Supposing that marshal had slipped into town from the rail head. Could be he was here now, right there in the saloon. Handful of men at his back, few useful guns, prospect of rewards for saving the gold. Men got to risking their skins for gold, even cold-sweat scared skins.

Reemer reached the clutter of crates and barrels at the rear of the bar, paused again to flick his gaze watchfully, left to right, then into the dark, staring windows of Mahooney's back room. Door there, he noted. Might be open; easy access to the bar; chance maybe to reckon the strength of town feeling, see just where that Marshal Quaid had holed up.

He had taken a half step, almost to the fringe of the shadows, when the door creaked, opened to no more than a chink and stayed there.

Reemer backed to the cover, licked his lips and fastened his stare on the shaft of gloom between door and jamb. Somebody watching, waiting, in no hurry to move. The door creaked again, opened a fraction wider, hovered, steadied on another creak. A hand on the knob, tight but uncertain, hesitating.

Reemer's eyes gleamed, fingers spreading like vines over the rim of his gun butt.

'Yuh goin' to move, or ain't yuh?' murmured Reemer to himself, flinching against a trickle of sweat in his neck, then stiffening as the bent, shuffling figure slid from the back room and paused to glance furtively over the shadows.

What the hell, a bar cleaning fellow, besom in one hand, Colt hanging loose in the other, apron tied tight at his waist, baggy pants scuffing at the dirt.

A soft grin flickered at Reemer's lips as he eased a shade to his left, waited for the fellow to part turn his back on him, then stepped clear of the crates and slung a stiff, grappling arm round the man's neck.

'Not a sound,' he grunted against Beanstalk's choking gasp of breath as he dragged him into the crates, kicking aside the dropped Colt and besom. 'How many in there? They got guns? That hearse left yet? Yuh seen a lawman name of Quaid?' The questions spilled from Reemer's mouth like chewed grit.

'I ain't nobody, mister,' spluttered Beanstalk, squirming under the arm lock. 'Just the cleaner here. I ain't seen nothin'.'

The arm tightened. 'Two minutes, that's all yuh got,' hissed Reemer into Beanstalk's ear, a waft of warm, stale breath settling like drizzle on his cheek. 'Two short minutes – and I'm countin'.'

'Hearse's headin' for the rail head,' croaked Beanstalk. 'I seen that. Right now. Sure it is.' He gulped. 'Yuh one of them raiders?'

'I ain't nobody to you, fella. Just get on with it. What about that lawman?'

'Ain't seen no lawman, nothin' like one, not since we had that sonofabitch, Hendy, runnin' the place.'

The arm lock gripped. 'How many back there?'

'Nobody of any count. Swear to it. Just m'self, coupla old-timers, fella drunk. . . . There ain't nobody, damn it. Town ain't for movin' none.' Beanstalk's eyes watered and swivelled in their sockets. 'I'm tellin' yuh, mister—'

'Yuh ain't tellin' me nothin', not no more yuh ain't,' growled Reemer, releasing the hold as he shoved Beanstalk deeper into the crates and watched him sink to a cringing heap. 'Yuh done your bit, fella,' he grinned, scraping his tongue across the back of his teeth. 'I'm obliged.'

'Now hold it there, fella. Just hold it, will yuh? I ain't nothin' to yuh – nothin' a deal to nobody – and I ain't for spoilin' in what yuh doin' here. Please y'self. Live and let live, what I say.' Beanstalk swallowed, sweated and stared glassy-eyed into the barrel of Reemer's probing Colt. 'Ain't no lawman here, never has been. Hendy said as how he was comin', but that was before. . . .' He swept a trembling hand over his matted hair. 'Hell, if yuh goin' to do it, do it. Ain't nobody here goin' to give a damn over likes of me.'

'Savin' me.'

The snapped, blade-sharp words came from somewhere deep in the shadows beyond Reemer, a steady, toneless voice that seemed to fall through the still, chilled air as if tossed out like a stone.

Reemer's stare flicked instantly from Beanstalk to the meaningless shapes and blurs of the suddenly fading night, narrowed to a slitted gleam, and glared.

'Who's "me"?' he hissed, flexing the Colt in his fingers.

'Been waitin' on me, it seems,' came the voice

again. 'But we already met, ain't we, back there, on the train.'

'Quaid!' snorted Reemer, his lips twitching on a glaze of saliva. 'Marshal Quaid.'

Beanstalk groaned and cringed deeper into a corner of the crates.

Reemer's fingers flexed again, the Colt in their grip lifting and levelling. 'I been waitin' – you bet,' he smiled.

'Pleasure's all mine, mister,' said Quaid. 'Time I got to settlin' with yuh. Good friend of mine'll be expectin' it.'

'Friend?' frowned Reemer. 'What yuh talkin' about?' The slitted glare shifted, skimming the shapes and half shadows for the slightest movement, stalling for the split-second of spotting it. 'I ain't for mixin' with the likes of lawman's friends.'

'Just killin' 'em, eh? Like yuh did Mr Brown.'

Reemer eased a slow, sliding step to his right, fingered the Colt anxiously, relaxed the smile to a cynical grin. 'Him?' he scoffed. 'Double-dealer. Fooled Friar some, that's for sure. But I spotted him. I *always* spot 'em, same as I spotted you in that corner seat – same as I'm spottin' yuh right now, mister.' The grin faded, the gun hand steadied. 'Wouldn't move if I were you. Be yuh last.'

Beanstalk moaned and screwed his eyes.

Reemer slid another step. 'I ain't gamblin' none on this, mister. Gotta busy day comin' up. Got m'self some Western Central gold to load!' The slanted glare widened, the gaze flicked, probed. 'Yuh hearin' me there, mister?'

The blaze roared across the silence like a spitting flare of flame, rolled an echo high and wide, shuddering, deafening and drowning Reemer's groan as the Colt spun crazily from his grip on the searing pain and bubbling blood at his thigh.

He spun round, a dazed, bewildered haze misting his eyes, twisting his lips, gushing a rush of saliva from his mouth. 'Yuh moved, damn yuh!' he groaned miserably. 'Yuh moved! Shouldn't have done that. . . .' He clawed wildly for the Colt.

'What yuh think yuh see ain't always what it is,' murmured Quaid, moving in on the man from the shadows behind him. 'Fool's gold, mister, fool's gold.' Four shots rang out, measured, aimed, timed, twisting Reemer's body through a scrambling lurch until he lay still, wide-eyed and bleeding.

'Joker,' grunted Quaid, holstering his smoking piece.

TWENTY-TWO

The shots rang out like the scratched cawing of angered crows. Charlie Hicks flinched and gulped on the tight, sticky grip of his collar; Morgan Friar reached instinctively for his low-slung Colt and slanted a pinched, gleaming gaze over the spreading lift of first light; a gunslinger at his side slid a step forward; another hissed through clenched teeth; a third glanced anxiously to the passenger car, swallowed, wiped the sweat from his cheeks and mouthed what most gathered there on the rail head were thinking:

'Just who in hell's doin' the shootin' down there?'

'Thought yuh said as how yuh'd heeled this town,' began his partner, flicking a wet, tired gaze to Friar.

'I have, damn yuh!' scowled Friar. 'That ain't town-folk shootin'. That's Reemer.' He turned to the men, a fast grin breaking his scowl. 'Doin' what he does best, ain't it? Flushin' out the rats.'

'Yuh mean that fella Quaid more like,' drawled a lounging, loose-hipped gunslinger, chewing on a wad of baccy.

Friar stiffened and turned to the spreading light. 'Mebbe, mebbe . . .' he murmured, then turned again. 'Don't matter none, does it? Another hour and we'll be through here. Put the whole place back of us. Get to the real business.'

'Hearse is movin' now. Down there. Just pullin' outa the street.'

Charlie Hicks flinched again and eased to the rear of the watching men, craning against his sticky collar for a sight of the trundling hearse as it grew on the dawn like a slow black beetle probing from its lair.

All looked just as it should, he thought, just as Friar was expecting: a town hearse, bent, creased undertaker at the reins behind the plodding team, drapes full closed, mournful silence, save for the scuff of hoofs, grind of old wheels, creak of leather and tack. A respectful last journey for the dearly departed. Damn it, anybody would figure for there being a dead body back there!

'Right, boys,' grinned Friar, his fingers drumming across his holster, 'open up that freight car. We start loadin' gold minute that hearse reins in.'

Charlie's neck sank into a swamp of collar and sweat.

'Town's playin' ball – hearse is comin' up now.' The hotel proprietor moved quickly along the passenger car, pausing at each window to squint and peer into the dusky, half-lit dawn.

'So who's goin' to do it?' croaked the cattleman, running a finger over the Colt on the table in front of him. 'I'm willin',' he added, raising his gaze to the faces watching him.

'Mebbe we should hold up some here,' said a gambler, lounging into a seat. 'Ain't goin' to achieve a deal with one gun to my thinkin'.'

'He's right,' drawled his partner, picking at the specks of dirt on his frock coat. 'Get y'self killed easy as spittin'.'

'Damnit, we take out that fella Friar there . . .' sweated the cattleman, flattening his hand on the Colt, his eyes bulging. 'Take him out and I wouldn't give two-bits for the others. Seen the Bar Nine boys do it times. Cut out the maverick and the herd calms soft as a babe. Never fails.'

'We ain't talkin' cattle here,' said the lounging gambler. 'We got some desperate fellas out there, and they ain't playin' for dirt stakes exactly.'

'So what *do* we do?' The proprietor reached the last window and peered closer. 'Yuh got about three minutes to decide.'

'Well, way I see it,' mouthed the frock-coated man, 'we should mebbe wait a while.'

'Wait, f'Cris'sake!' flared the cattleman. 'What we waitin' for? Been *waitin'* since this heap of iron pulled into town. Any more waitin' and we'll be all waitin' on that hearse cartin' us to Boot Hill!'

The snivelling girl blew her nose into an already sodden handkerchief and moaned. The pale-faced man hugged the valise closer to him and gulped. The colonel's wife came to her feet in a flurry of skirts and lace and stamped her foot.

'Good thing you men aren't standin' to the lives of others,' she snapped. 'We'd all be dead by now! Here, give me the gun.'

'Now steady there, ma'am,' said the cattleman. 'Appreciate how yuh feelin' and yuh daughter there along of yuh, but—'

'Oh, stop your frettin',' snapped the woman again. 'You don't think I've been married to the colonel all these years just to keep his bed warm, do you?' The snivelling daughter squeaked. 'Know a sight more about firearms and usin' them than you'll ever get to, mister. Now, give me the gun.'

'And just who yuh goin' to shoot, lady?' asked a gambler.

'Why, Mr Friar, of course. Who else?'

'Sure, just like that. Yuh walk right up to him there and ask him real polite if he'd mind standin' still while yuh kill him! Call that smart, lady?'

'I do indeed,' huffed the woman. 'Smart, and *practical*. I doubt if Mr Friar is likely to be expectin' me to walk out of this car, is he? Last person he'd figure for.'

'But, lady—' blustered the cattleman.

The girl began to sob and squeak again.

'Do stop that, Letitia!' The woman stiffened and shuffled the folds of her skirts. 'Do I get the gun, or don't I?'

Lacy Alice eased to the bounce of the hearse and tightened her grip on the soft, sweat-soaked hand of the girl huddled next to her. She blinked on the darkness and sniffed again at the sweet, scent-laden air of the wagon. Lingering smell of death and the dead in freshly planed pine here, she thought, sensing the response of the soft hand. Appropriate enough, if you happened to see the irony of it.

'T'ain't every day yuh get to ridin' live in one of these!' whispered a bar girl facing her.

'Just so long as yuh got a return ticket!' quipped another to the murmur of nervous giggles.

Alice shushed for quiet and widened her eyes on the gloom. 'Yuh all know what to do?' she asked softly. 'Use yuh gun best yuh know how. Just keep firin', all right?'

'Prayin' along of it,' said a girl.

'Darn sight too late for prayin' when yuh get to ridin' a hearse!'

'Mebbe somebody'll be prayin' for us.'

'We ain't alone,' hissed Alice. 'There'll be others, you bet on it. Just do like I say and mebbe we'll all be sleepin' easy in our beds come t'morrow.'

'I ain't *slept* easy in a bed in years,' giggled a girl in the corner.

'I just ain't slept!' drawled a tired voice.

'All right, all right,' urged Alice. 'Let's have some quiet, eh? Don't want them scum out there knowin' what's waitin' on 'em.' She reached to balance herself against a creaking roll. 'Almost there. Get y'selves set. And remember, shoot straight, shoot fast.' A slow smile trembled at her lips. 'Good luck.'

The hand in her grip grew hotter.

Charlie Hicks had already backed as close to the platform of the passenger car as he dared without raising Friar's attention by the time the hearse had drawn up at the far end of the rail head. Only one place for his duty now, he reckoned: with his train and the fare-paying folk riding it. Rail company would expect it of him; stand to the passengers at all costs; folk first, freight last. Rule of the railroad in Charlie's book.

Even so, having got here, three steps short of boarding the car with hardly a glance from Friar or his sidekicks, what to do now? Clamber aboard, seal the door, get the folk flat again on the floor, or see it out right here, simply waiting on the gunslingers turning their iron on all witnesses?

Or would the surprise awaiting Friar back of the hearse's closed drapes be enough?

Hell, two of Friar's men making their way to the hearse right now, moving through the soft break of first light like a couple of early hounds nosing out the night's leftovers; Colts drawn, taking no chances, not even against the wizened old body of the under-taker seated there in the driving seat.

Charlie dug a finger deep into the collar of his shirt, swallowed, glanced hurriedly at Friar supervis-ing the unloading of the crates from the freight car to the platform, and was another step closer to the compartment when the sweat in his neck began to run ice-cold across his shoulders.

One of the drapes at the hearse had moved, blinked like a waking eye, shifted the merest fraction for the soft, levelled probe of a barrel.

Charlie swallowed, sweated in the grip of the collar, limbs suddenly heavy and unmoving, gaze riveted on the drape, the gap, the barrel, and then, in the flick of his eyes, on the approaching sidekicks.

Had they seen the shift, the glint of steel? They were still moving at the same pace, easing in no hurry through the dapple of light, shadows sprawling ahead of them. Maybe they were concentrating on the undertaker, watching for him to make the twitch that might hint at a trap. Last thing they would be reckoning on would be a hearse-load of tousle-haired bar girls all of a lather for a frenzied shoot-out.

More growled orders from Friar. The thump of crates to the platform; scuffing of boots; bodies bent to the manhandling of a fortune.

A movement at Charlie's back, flitting across the corner of his gaze. Somebody stepping to the passenger car platform. Damn it, had the folk back there no notion of their very lives being within a hair's-breadth of oblivion if they so much as lifted a finger? All it would take was for Friar, one of his men. . . .

But all it took in the next ear-shattering, light-spinning seconds for the morning to shatter like the splintering of glass and the air to fill with the creep of smoke and the smell of cordite, was the searing blaze of lead from the hearse and the whooping screams of the bodies it had carted.

TWENTY-THREE

Friar spun from the freight car and into the cover of the unloaded crates at the first whipping crack of shots, cursing as he crashed to the platform and too bewildered in the next half-minute to take in anything of the mayhem erupting around him, save for the scurry of bodies, the darting, tumbling shapes of his men and the blaze and roar of frenzied shooting.

Charlie Hicks tumbled to the passenger-car platform, his gaze blurred, mouth open on a shout that died in his throat, one arm outstretched for a hold on the platform rail, the fingers of the clawing hand finding only the frills of the colonel's wife's dress as she toppled towards him, a Colt waving wildly in her grip.

'What the hell!' he groaned, pushing the woman back to the door of the car where the cattleman and the hotel proprietor hovered like nodding, bent-necked birds.

One of Friar's men crashed from the freight car in a flurry of arms and legs and raced to the edge of the platform, his face gleaming, eyes wide and wet as watering moons and stared for a moment in pale disbelief at the sprawled bodies of the sidekicks who had approached the hearse.

In the next he lay dead to the hail of flying lead from the bar girls' raging barrels.

Gus Smalley spat and pounded his leaden legs over the dirt from the last of the old shacks to Clancy Springs' burned-out wagons, dropped to one knee, raised a Winchester to his shoulder and fired fast and hard at a scuttling sidekick. The fellow halted in a cloud of dust, groaned and spread his fingers through the bubbling blood at his bicep.

Gus grunted, left the man to stagger away to the shadows and ranged the rifle for the next target.

Morgan Friar cursed again, cleared the sweat from his eyes and raised himself gingerly from the cover of the crate.

'Sonofabitch,' he mouthed, scanning his gaze from the freight car to the gun-smoking, open drapes of the hearse. Three of his men down he could count to, no sign of Reemer, and that whore-boss, Alice, holding the ground out there like some over-zealous platoon captain.

He swung his gaze to the passenger car and was figuring the half-dozen paces it would take to reach it, when a Colt spat from the near window, winging a blaze of lead to within inches of his head before burying itself in the crate. Hell, he thought, licking his lips, a gun in there too! But how and whose? Buried in that woman's skirts, or that pale-faced fellow's bag? Damn it, should have checked.

He ducked again at another volley of fire from the hearse and began to shuffle slowly on his heels to the darkness of the station office, his hand slipping like a melting shadow from the crate of gold.

Joe Fane twanged his braces hard against his chest and heard his stomach grumble like a churning barrel. He flicked his gaze anxiously to Bart Jessom's face and peered for a sight of his eyes behind the glinting rash of sweat.

'Hell, yuh see that?' he rasped. 'Lacy Alice and the girls . . . right there, in the hearse, guns an' all.'

'Always was a wild thing,' mumbled Bart as if talking into space.

'So what we do now?' asked Joe, hitching his trousers.

'We do like Quaid said – get to them passengers.'

'Through that? All that flyin' lead. Hell, we'll be crow meat in two steps.'

'We do it, Joe. Now. Cross the rail and come up on the car blind side. Follow me.'

They went towards the track like skipping midges.

Lacy Alice shivered, relaxed the Colt in the droop of her skirt between her legs and blew at a straggle of hair across her face as she twisted to the 'breed girl at her side. For somebody who had never handled a gun before she was performing there like a professional.

'Yuh gettin' the hang of it?' she grinned, watching the girl tighten her two-handed grip on the piece as she levelled it to a target.

'This is all for Mr Brown,' murmured the girl, screwing one eye to the aim. 'I owe him.'

Alice stiffened and grimaced at the roar of the shot, then slid a hand to the girl's arm. 'Hold it,' she called. 'Hold yuh fire, gals. Let's take stock of the damage.'

'Three down, the rest scattered,' piped a voice.

'Four if yuh take count of the one squirmin' back

of the burned wagons,' came another voice.

'Had a sight of Gus out there, and somebody fired from inside the passenger car.'

'Anybody see the undertaker?' asked the girl at Alice's back, her gaze swinging quickly over the smoke-hazed, breaking morning.

'Flat as a board right beneath us! And still breathin'.'

'Right, so now we shift,' said Alice, brushing her hair to her neck. 'Get ourselves outa this coffin and into fresh air. We head for the wagons, fast and low. Don't wait for nothin'.'

The girls nodded and began to move, easing through the door of the hearse to the ground like a fluttering glide of moths as their skirts swung clear to the open space.

Alice was the last to leave and the first, as her buttoned boots scuffed the dirt, to pause and probe the fading night shadows and the lift of the day shapes taking their place as if expecting something to move. But there was nothing, she thought, cringing against the keener air, not unless you figured for the sudden silence being a presence.

The soft steps of Marshal Quaid?

Morgan Friar waited, tense as a fly under threat of being crushed, seeming to not so much as breathe as his eyes shifted over the gloom of the station office, his gun hand easy to the touch of the holstered Colt.

Too much silence now, he mused; no shouts from his men, no movement among the passengers, no footfalls, shots, and nothing of Reemer. He swallowed slowly and backed on, one short step at a time, to the door at the rear, stepping carefully over the sprawled body of Sam Wards in the skim of drying blood, senses raw-edged but only half concentrated against the swirl of his thoughts and images.

No wagons and now no hearse, and maybe no chance of the gold being moved, not without men, even one man. Even, damn it, Reemer, for all his fretting. So maybe now was the time for settling matters on a strictly personal level: take what he could, when and however it came to hand, sooner the better, forget the boys, dead or alive – forget Reemer if need be – shoot to kill when the need arose and put the rail head and Peaceway behind him before morning was full up and the sun a step higher.

Cut the losses, he decided, his hand reaching slowly for the door latch, and bury the mistakes. Too many of them: that double-dealing fellow, Brown, Lacy Alice and her bar girls, the townfolk he had let live, the hearse he should have organized himself, passengers he should have shot. . . .

One in particular.

He paused, the hand still a reach from the latch, and turned slowly to the curtain of gloom at his back. Seemed like it was following in his every step, faceless but watching, breathing but silent. Might almost have been a real body, he thought.

Quaid?

He was getting jumpy, could feel the tiredness creeping behind his eyes, scratching at his limbs. He grunted and licked his lips. This was no place to be, not like this, not for a man the nature of Morgan Friar who had never in his life scurried into hiding from a man with a gun. Not even Marshal Quaid.

Especially not Quaid!

He opened the door and passed softly, silently

down the few steps to the cluttered loading bay, slid to the deepest shadow, waited and watched.

Soft groan from somewhere out there of a wounded man; clang of a door in the passenger car; snort of a horse at the hearse. He moved, one patch of shadow to the next, narrowed his gaze on the cracking canopy of light, the fingering shafts of sun, then eased it wider to the emerging sprawl of the street and the soft swirl of swept dust from the board-walk fronting Mahooney's bar.

'Sonofabitch!' he droned, at the sight of Beanstalk's besom going about its chores as it would on any morning. He cursed again, watched the barman finish the job with an extravagant flourish, half turn to the batwings before pausing, raising a hand to shield his eyes to the gathering glare and staring deep into the street.

It took Morgan Friar just five short, sweat-soaking seconds to put a shape and a face to the firm, measured steps of the approaching blur.

'Not so simple, Marshal,' he murmured to himself, the tips of his fingers skimming the butt of his Colt, 'but yuh sure as hell welcome to try!'

Friar waited another two minutes in the shadows of the bay before slipping like one of them into the tumbledown cover of the old shacks. Quiet enough here, he reckoned, and nothing moving at the rail head; almost as if somebody had passed out the word for calm, silence, a time to pause and wait.

Maybe somebody very like the man walking out of the morning's first dusty glare as if he owned the street he trod, as if there was nothing there in that slow stirring town to raise so much as a spit of sweat.

Not even the threat of Lud Reemer.

Reemer was dead, thought Friar, pressing his shoulders tight to the wall of a shack, a nerve twitching high on his temple. And no guesses needed to name the fellow whose hand had been on the gun. Only Quaid would step from a train, melt to the night and be there like a ghost come sun-up.

Only Quaid . . . the steps of him dogging a man's life till he got to wondering if the fellow was his own shadow. Only Quaid . . . always coming on, never forgetting, never giving up; always a score to be settled, no matter how long it might take, where or when it might be.

'Damn you, Marshal!' hissed Friar, shifting his gaze to the street again, but stiffening instantly, the gun hand flat to the Colt. Nothing of Quaid now. No blur of the man against the soft glare, no shape in the settling scuffs of dust. Nothing of the barman on the boardwalk. Nothing of anybody, damn it, but the eyes were still there. He could feel them.

'Yuh out there, Quaid?' called Friar in a rasping, crackling voice, the words like bulges as they left his throat. 'I ain't for stalkin' about none. No cat-and-mouse, eh? Straight up, same as we both know it. What yuh say?'

Silence, and still nothing moving.

'Don't get to dwellin' on it, will yuh? Time's runnin' out. Somebody's gotta shift that train.' Friar swallowed and blinked on his watering eyes. 'How'd yuh get to figurin' all this, anyhow? Tip off – that how yuh knew I was here and why? That'd be it, wouldn't it? Sure, 'cus yuh don't never give up, do yuh? That yuh don't. No way. . . .'

He swallowed again, slid a warm, sticky hand over

the holster, the fingers drumming lightly, thumb stiff and flat. 'Yuh send that fella, Brown, ahead of yuh? Here to keep a watch, was he, stay in step till yuh got here? Nice fella. Yuh should've seen him take out that two-bit Sheriff Hendy. Did yuh real proud. Shame Reemer got to fidgetin' like he did, but I guess yuh taken care of him, eh? Don't see him about. . . .'

Friar shifted, risked a glance from the wall of the shack towards the street and the still empty, silent dirt around it. So just where was Quaid now?

'Still, done yuh a favour here, ain't I? Got shut of Hendy, cleaned up the town in a manner of speakin'. Could almost reckon for yuh owin' me. But I ain't greedy, so what say we cut the feudin' from all these years and get to sharin' that gold sittin' back there? See us easy in our old age, wouldn't it? Fifty-fifty and we both ride out?'

Friar's hand dropped firm and steady to the butt of the Colt, drew it, let it hover barrel skywards for a moment but was levelled and already blazing as he sprang from the cover of the wall, the shots wild and rapid in a searing, echoing roar.

'Have it your way if yuh want, o'course,' he yelled, spinning on his heels, the Colt loose aimed and smoking in his grip. 'Winner here takes all!'

He spun to the left, to the right, gathered himself in a crouching stance, eyes gleaming like pinpricks of a hidden light in the search for a shape, a movement.

'Quaid, damn yuh!'

He had stretched a hand to the wall for support, the Colt levelled again, the sweat like a dousing of drizzle across his face, when the misty, dust-speckled light ahead of him at the loading bay was torn apart as if in the grip of angry hands.

'Too many towns to count, too many dead to number.'

The voice seemed to gather from somewhere beyond the shape of the man, lift on the thin morning air, then gnash across the space like the grinding of teeth.

Friar raged the Colt, high, wide and crazy in its frenzied aim, till the chamber spun empty and his fingers were scrambling for a hold on the blade in his belt.

'Whole heap of a bad life and the livin' of it, ain't it, Morgan?' said Quaid coming on through the first shimmer of the glare. 'But I heard what yuh were callin' back there, and you're right: weren't the gold that bothered me, it was you, just like it's always been.'

He halted, his gun held loose at his side. 'And here yuh are and here am I. Timely, ain't it? But like yuh say, shame about Mr Brown, so this is for him.' He fired, fast and easy from the hip. 'And all the rest, 'til this piece spins free, is for the ghosts I got standin' to me. Yuh'll be dead when the last of 'em walks over yuh, Morgan, but yuh'll see 'em all where you're goin'.'

Marshal Quaid's Colt was still blazing when Engine 37's whistle shrieked across the morning to drown a dying man's curses.

TWENTY-FOUR

'Some places you don't ever want to see again – and we just pulled out of one of them!' The colonel's wife stiffened in her seat against the sway of the train, trimmed the pleated ruffles of the dress at her wrists, and sniffed loudly. 'What my husband will have to say about this, I shudder to think. Why, I wouldn't be one bit surprised if he don't—'

'Just be grateful to see yuh alive, ma'am,' clipped a gambler, raising one eye from the cards in his hand.

'Or not!' mumbled his partner behind a careful grunt.

'I just figure for us bein' real fortunate,' sighed the hotel proprietor. 'And there's a whole stack of folk back there we should be thankin'.'

'Say that again,' said the cattleman, flicking at a passing fly. 'Them bar girls for a start. Some shootin', eh? More to frills than meets the eye!'

The colonel's daughter giggled under the scorching glare of her mother.

'And them fellas who came to help us – Mr Fane and Mr Jessom. Real solid townfolk. Somebody should get to rewardin' 'em.' The proprietor

155

adjusted the fall of his jacket. 'Same goes for the conductor – showed he had guts there – and the engineer. Yessir, a whole stack.' He sighed again. 'Just one helluva shame about the men who died.'

'A whole sight more if it hadn't been for that marshal,' murmured a gambler. 'Him yuh gotta thank for this old iron horse still rollin'.'

'And yuh can say *that* again,' said the cattleman, still watching the fly. 'Same mould as the Bar Nine boys: fearless, fast, just got to doin' what he had to do. And still doin' it. Out there now with the conductor, and still watchin'.'

'But what happened to the little man with the bag?' asked the colonel's wife. 'We still have his Colt.'

'Last I seen of him he was slinkin' off into town,' smiled a gambler. 'Mebbe he liked the look of the place.'

'Well, he's welcome!' huffed the woman, turning to stare out of the window.

The gambler shrugged and winked at the girl who, with a soft, engaging blush, wriggled and winked back.

Charlie Hicks blinked against the rush of air across the passenger-car platform, consulted his timepiece and pocketed it again with a pronounced grunt. 'Night train's goin' to be a whole day late,' he sighed, glancing quickly at the man resting easy with the sway of the car. 'Not that anyone's goin' to complain, least of all the bank,' he added, tapping the timepiece. 'But when I get to thinkin'. . . .' He sighed again. 'Best not to, I reckon. Tell yuh somethin', though, this'll go down in railroad history, and I ain't foolin'. They'll be tellin' it for generations. But mebbe not all of it, eh, Marshal? Some things best not told.'

'Such as?' said Quaid, his gaze narrowed tight against the rushing air.

'Who it was tipped yuh off about Friar, what he planned, where he would be and when. Some fella with a grudge?'

'He had that sure enough. Friar had blinded him in a gang shoot-out, but he'd kept tabs on the scum and got to hear how he was plannin' on makin' the gold heist. I was trailin' that gunslinger, Jameson, when I crossed the fella and he told me what he'd heard. Made my own "arrangements" from there.'

Charlie waited a moment, his fingers tapping lightly on the timepiece. 'Can't speak high enough about yuh deputy, but, damn it, he shouldn't have died like that.'

'Did his job best he knew how. He wouldn't have wanted it other.'

'Well,' sighed Charlie, running a finger round his collar, 'I just hope the folk back there in Peaceway get to appreciatin' it. Good men died for 'em. . . . And, heck, if they don't get to makin' somethin' of that town of theirs. . . .' He straightened and patted his paunch. 'I'll be watchin', you bet on it. Train won't pull into Peaceway without me takin' a real close look.'

'Not too close,' murmured Quaid, putting the glow to a long cheroot. 'Best let the ghosts sleep easy.'

Charlie grunted and reached for his timepiece again. 'Say,' he grinned, 'we could be makin' up time here. Now ain't that somethin?'

But Marshal Quaid seemed not to be listening as his gaze scanned the sprawl of the empty horizon.

Maybe he was just thinking, mused Charlie, or just simply watching.

Hard to tell in a man like Quaid.

'All that gold – tell yuh, I ain't never seen so much,' said Joe Fane, raising his wide-eyed gaze to the saloon bar ceiling as his thumbs slid the length of his braces. 'Not never, I ain't. Can yuh imagine what a fella could do with gold like that?'

'Can see what he'd fast become,' quipped Lacy Alice, sidling from the cluttered table to the bar. 'Should get y'self a mirror, Joe.'

'Hell, no, not me,' grinned Joe. 'Why, if I had gold like I seen back there—'

'But yuh ain't and yuh ain't never goin' to,' drawled Bart Jessom, helping himself to another measure from a half-empty bottle. 'And the matter ain't for discussin', not when there's enough pine clutterin' Boot Hill to plant a forest. Ain't respectful, Joe, and that's the truth of it. We got matters a whole lot more pressin' to figure on.'

'Bart's right,' said Gus Smalley, lifting his feet for the swish of Beanstalk's besom. 'Time we woke up, got to lookin' where we are, *who* we are, and what we're goin' to do with the bits we got left.' His boots thudded back to the floor. 'Ain't a deal to pride ourselves on, is there?'

'We ain't got Hendy, that's for sure!' said Joe, slapping his braces to his shoulders.

'And we ain't got ourselves to thank for it neither,' snapped Bart. 'Fella we beat up and would've hanged soon as spit did that for us, and only 'cus a murderin' sonofabitch teamed along of him and forced his hand. And if it hadn't been for Marshal Quaid gettin'' here and Alice and the girls showin' a whole sight more guts than most of us, I'd reckon for this town bein' dead as them bodies up there on the Hill.' He finished the drink in a single gulp. 'There's more ghosts here than the livin' – and I ain't sure sometimes which is which!'

'Well, I am,' said Alice, stretching her arms along the bar as she leaned back on it. 'More than sure. We're goin' to do just like Quaid said before he climbed aboard that train. We're goin' to put this town to rights, beginnin' with you wearin' the law badge, Gus – no arguin' – and you, Joe, gettin' a new livery up and runnin', while Bart there opens his store and puts a decent discount to his goods till the town finds its feet. Me – I'm the new owner of this bar you're drinkin' in and the chairs you're sittin' on. Girls'll be helpin' me, and no favours on account and no messin'. So what yuh say?'

'Fine by me, Miss Alice,' smiled Beanstalk

'Well . . .' began Gus.

'I ain't never discounted nothin'!' croaked Bart.

'Oh, sure,' scoffed Joe, stretching his braces, 'and I suppose Marshal Quaid told yuh how we're goin' to pay for all this?'

'No, he didn't,' said Alice, her eyes narrowing. 'Just said as how we should get off our butts and do somethin' decent. And yuh can bet yuh sweet life he'll be back lookin' for it.' She paused. 'Owe it to him and his deputy, don't we?'

'Meantime,' scoffed Joe, 'we just get to hopin' for some real charitable Samaritan to step up here—'

The batwings creaked to the soft, finger touch of the pale-faced man peering over them. 'Excuse me,' he murmured nervously, shuffling into the bar, the valise clutched tight across his chest, 'don't wanna interrupt nothin' here, but I was wondering. . . . Happened to be one of the folk aboard the train back there . . . travellin' West, kinda lookin' for some place to settle, make an investment.

'Oh, I got the funds, sure enough, right here in my bag . . . dollar bills, bonds, all honestly come by. Got a business flair, I guess. Figured them fellas might have helped themselves . . . good as offered it, but nobody seemed interested. Anyhow, like the look of the town here, and you folk are sure as hell deservin' of real prospects, doin' what yuh did, so I was wonderin' . . . .'

It was the longest sun-filled minute in Peaceway's history before anybody spoke.